THE FINAL REVEAL

SEALs of Steel, Book 8

Dale Mayer

Books in This Series:

THE FINAL REVEAL: SEALS OF STEEL, BOOK 8
Dale Mayer
Valley Publishing Ltd.

Copyright © 2019

ISBN-13: 978-1-773360-88-1
Print Edition

About This Book

This is a novella tying up the SEALs of Steel series.

A prosthetic design engineer, Kat Greenwald is in love with Badger Horley.

The former SEALs team leader is the love of her life. But she's seen and heard firsthand of the fears and commitment issues Badger and his closest friends—once part of Navy special operations teams—struggle with on a daily basis. During their weekly get-togethers, the women in love with these former SEALs open up to each other about their longing to tie the knot and start families.

More than two years ago, Badger was badly injured after the truck his eight-man unit were in hit an antitank landmine. While he and his team have finally discovered the truth behind that devastating set-up, Badger sees the reality of his precarious future. His health could decline at any moment and he wants Kat to know exactly where the door to get out is if and when it does. The last thing he wants to do is invite pity, especially where the woman he loves is concerned. In a perfect world, he would have proposed to her the day they met. In the world he lives in, he can only conclude that harboring fears are always better than regrets.

But Kat isn't the type of woman to fear hard times and she's willing to take a leap of faith as far out into the unknown as she can get if it means her most fervent wish comes true.

Sign up to be notified of all Dale's releases here!
http://dalemayer.com/category/blog/

PROLOGUE

KAT SAT CURLED on the couch in Badger's place, their home. Dennis—Allison's brother with the Santa Fe Police Department—had just left. Everybody else remained here, after giving their statements. Dennis would get them typed up; then they'd have to sign them. As far as Kat was concerned, this six-week long nightmare was finally over. Even longer actually. She couldn't believe how far Badger and his unit had come in such a short time.

She curled up against Badger's side, petting Dotty. She'd moved into his house weeks ago. It felt as much like her own as it felt like his now. As if she'd come home. Dotty apparently approved too. Kat still had her house, and it was rented out. She wasn't sure what to do with it long-term. At the moment, she wasn't planning on making that decision.

So much had happened in such a short time. She knew she wanted one more thing to happen, but Badger was still dealing with commitment issues. He would have a lifetime of physical problems, and he figured he didn't want her to be beholden to him. She thought his logic was stupid, as love was about taking care of each other, regardless of what happened. *In sickness and in health*, as the wedding vows go.

As she sat next to him, a plan formed in the back of her mind. She half straightened up, caught Badger's questioning look and then sagged back down again. She didn't dare let him know what she was thinking. Someone like Badger needed some things to happen without his involvement.

She looked over at Honey and Allison, the two women she could see from where she sat. Allison, a cop like her brother, was a hell of an addition to the group. Seven men, seven women. Who knew such a thing was possible and all so fast? Some of them had known each other longer, like Clary and Talon, like herself and Badger. Even like Honey and Erick in a manner. Yet the others—Jager and Allison; Geir and Morning; Lazlo and Minx; Cade and Faith—had never met before this Mouse hunt started. But sometimes the good things happened fast.

"So is this done now? Everybody got their questions answered?" Kat asked lazily. "I'd say we could put it to rest, but I think we probably all still need to talk about it for a few days or so until we finally wind down."

"The conversation will probably continue for a while," Jager said quietly. "I've got the main answers I needed. I just didn't realize how twisted a person can become."

Allison nodded. She was tucked up against his side, her head against his shoulder.

Kat looked at Jager and smiled. "Speaking of decisions, I took another look at your file and I think I can help you get more mobility with more advanced prosthetics."

Jager's face lit up.

She held up a cautionary hand. "We'll have to do some measurements and getting the right design could take time. You were the only one of the unit I didn't think I could help, now, however ... I have an idea that might work."

Jager reached out a hand and Kat grasped it, gave it a gentle squeeze, then turned her attention to Allison. "You have decisions to make too, don't you?"

Allison chuckled. "They've been coming hard and fast ever since I met Jager. Not just about a place to live but also about what I want to do with my life."

"Oh, don't we love those major decisions we're forced to make from time to time?" Morning said on a chuckle. She leaned forward. "I know this isn't really related or anything, but I just heard from the San Diego gallery owner. He's superthrilled and has already presold the four paintings I took in."

"Presold?" Badger asked in surprise.

Morning nodded. "He showed them to a private collector, and he wanted all four of them. The thing is, the amount of money the gallery owner charged was just incredible. I'm still in shock. I didn't know people would pay that much."

"It was still too cheap," Geir said, chuckling. "Your work will be worth way more soon."

"I don't know what art is worth," Honey said. "I don't have an artistic bone in my body, but I really admire people who can create beautiful paintings. The buyer obviously felt that way too."

Morning chuckled. "I don't know how beautiful they are. I've certainly got some pressure on me now to create more for the show in the fall, but he charged over ten grand a painting. Honestly, I'm dumbfounded."

"Wow. Did you basically make a teacher's annual salary by selling four paintings?" Kat asked.

"Go, you!" Honey cried out.

Morning beamed. "I know, right? It seems unbelievable."

"I think all of us have come to a point where some decisions definitely need to be made," Cade said lazily. He was sprawled on a big armchair, with Faith half lying on him, half beside him. "It's been a hell of a ride. But I, for one, am so grateful to get off."

"Hear, hear. It's been six weeks since Badger *badgered* us to go to England," Talon said with a grin. "That's just a little too unbelievable."

"I know, right?" Badger shook his head. "But not even I understood what we would find at the end of this. It breaks my heart. Mouse had seemed to be such a good kid."

Minx—Mouse's childhood friend—had been even more traumatized than the others over last night's episode. "He was a good kid, but he became a very broken man. It'll take me a while to grieve for the loss of the boy I knew."

"It'll take all of us time to grieve," Laszlo said with a quiet smile. "We have to understand that who we thought Mouse was, he wasn't, and we need to lay to rest that version of the man we believed in." Lazlo sighed. "We also need to follow-up with Mason about Mouse impersonating Ryan Hanson and Poppy hacking into the navy's database."

"So much planning to maneuver himself into his dream career," Badger said, "just because he didn't want to put in the time and effort to try to make it on his own merit. And all those senseless deaths …"

"The thing is, as we all know, very few make it through BUD/S," Geir said. "The training is brutal. The endurance required is horrific, and Mouse probably knew he didn't have what it took if he tried the normal way. But he had spent a lifetime getting what he wanted in other ways. That's why his relationship with Poppy lasted so long. Poppy had been in the navy, still had connections. Poppy hadn't been a SEAL himself, like he had told Mouse, but Poppy had access to a lot of people to help Mouse's agenda. And, sadly, money buys almost anything."

"Mouse took such a chance though," Kat said. "To blow up a military transport truck and expect to walk away uninjured is asking a lot."

"I know," Badger said. "And it always bothered me that he was the one who had supposedly died in our land mine accident. I never heard much about his injuries. I should have followed up on it. We never did talk to the medics, and we never knew about the man who switched the bodies."

"He didn't have to switch bodies. He just had to switch tags," Erick said. "And you know what Afghanistan was like for our troops, dealing with our dead over there. This accomplice of Mouse's in some makeshift desert morgue could have chosen from any number of corpses, picked the one most likely and switched out a toe tag. Nobody knew. Nobody cared. I don't know if we'll ever sort out that mess. As far as Ryan's family goes, it'll be a shock for them to find out the truth."

"I wonder if the brass will take this down to the truth?" Laszlo asked. "We need to do what we can to recover Ryan's body and have the soldier buried properly for his family's sake."

"And that is a thread I do want closure on," Geir said. "It's not fair for that family to not know."

"Agreed, but we may never locate him unless something in Poppy's laptop reveals that information," Cade said. "And that is certainly possible, since Poppy loved to document everything. It'll take weeks, if not months, to comb through all that evidence. Including stuff about Poppy's relationships, shall we call them. And he had plenty. Most of them were much less than savory."

"Mouse was always very focused," Minx said. "It's hard

to see his dedication and determination focused on something so wrong."

"I don't think that was it at all," Talon stated. "Mouse had a fantasy, a dream, but he was focused on being something other than what he was capable of. He wanted to be a SEAL, something that made him smile, that he could be proud of. Even if he didn't do the work himself, he had convinced himself he still was a SEAL. And when it was all about to blow up in his face, he had to do something to keep from being exposed as the fraud he was. The easiest way out was to fake his death, take himself out with an honorable funeral. But to live through an explosion and to endure rehab only then to come after us again,... that's just twisted."

Kat hopped to her feet, Dotty jumped up with her. "I'm going to make a big pitcher of iced tea. Then I'm going for a swim in the pool. The conversation here is rough and heavy."

"Are there any salads left from last night?" Badger asked.

She nodded. "And, if need be, we can come up with other food for lunch too."

Immediately the conversation lightened.

KAT SMILED AS she walked into the kitchen. Badger's house was fantastic. And it was great for having big gatherings like this. She put on the teakettle, and, instead of opening the fridge to check for more food, she opened the double glass doors and headed outside to the pool. Dotty bounced across the green grass in delight.

A huge grassy area was on the far side. Kat wondered

how that would work for what she had planned. And how much could she plan alone?

She shook her head. She would need help with this. She sent Stone a text. He'd long been a patient of hers and had often said, if she needed anything, to just call. Well, this might not be what he expected, but she was *calling*. **I need help.**

What do you need? You know I'm here for you.

I need help with something for a few months down the road. It'll take that long to plan this out.

Plan out what?

She chuckled and explained in as few words as possible. **Are you in?**

Hell no came back his instant response.

She laughed out loud. **Chicken?**

Hell yes. That's taking a path with massive repercussions.

She was still amused when she sent Ice a quick text. **I need help.**

Ice responded. **What's up?**

I have a plan. I'm thinking three months down the road.

What kind of a plan?

She explained.

Instantly Ice's response came back. **I'm in. Don't worry. I'll get Levi to help too.**

Kat glanced inside at the group seated in the living room and started to laugh. She was still laughing as she walked back inside.

Badger looked at her. "What are you up to?"

She smoothed out her expression and smiled at him. "Nothing. What could I possibly be up to?"

He studied her face and frowned. "You look like you're

hiding something. And, in my world, that means trouble."

"I guess you'll have to wait and see."

She gazed over the backyard. It was definitely big enough for a wedding.

CHAPTER 1

A WEEK LATER Kat walked into the room, whistling. Badger looked at her suspiciously. She just beamed. Had been since she started toying with this wedding idea.

"You still haven't told me what you're up to," he said mildly.

She gave him an innocent look. "I'm up to nothing. Can't I just be happy?"

He groaned. "I've asked you a dozen times what's going on, but each time you've given me the same answer."

"So maybe by now you should believe me." She chuckled and sat down on the lounger beside him. "Did I ever tell you how much I love your house?"

"At least twice a day," he said blandly. He reached out a hand.

She slid her hand in his and sat back. "It's really nice to have a peaceful haven to come home to at the end of the day."

"You are looking more tired today." The worry in his voice was obvious.

She shook her head. "Oh, no you don't. No starting to worry about me. I'm fine," she said firmly.

"*Starting* has nothing to do with it," he said with a chuckle. "I've always been worried about you."

She smiled, her head rolling to the side so she could

study his lean chiseled features. "It's just me worrying about you. Making sure you don't overdo anything."

He smiled. "I have something—no," he corrected. "I have everything to live for."

She smiled. "I'm really glad to hear you say that. For a long time I wasn't so sure."

"I know. But it's all good now." He reached down to massage his stump.

"How is it?" She walked a fine line between worrying and nagging. They'd both lived independently for a long time. Looking after and worrying about someone else was both unique and richly rewarding.

"Achy. And itchy."

"Both of those are good signs."

He smiled. "Only you'd say that." He looked over at her prosthetic. "Was it hard for you to get used to it?"

"For me it was a blessing. I was dragging around a non-functioning limb, and it was getting in my way. I kept injuring it, kept breaking it, and all I really wanted was freedom from something holding me back."

"Interesting. I guess in that sense, it released you from a prison."

"Exactly. Too often people feel like they're in a prison once they get a prosthetic. It's one of the reasons I went into the business I did. There's a need for a huge mind-set change."

"You've been great for all of us."

"The feeling is mutual." Out of the blue, she announced, "I don't feel like cooking tonight."

"It's Friday. We can go out if you want."

She shook her head. "Nah, I don't think so. Maybe order in though."

"Yeah, what you got in mind?" he asked. "We've always got to feed our appetite in bed too."

She laughed, her voice ringing out free and happy. "Men and sex."

"I didn't hear any protest out of you last night." His grin was wide. "Or this morning."

"Only that I had to make it to work on time so my clients weren't waiting for me." She chuckled.

"We've got a good life here, don't we?"

"Yeah, we sure do."

"I still have to figure out what I want to do with my life."

"Nope," she said. "I think you all have to figure out what you all will do together."

He glanced at her. "I'm not sure some group venture will work."

"I'm not sure something apart will work. The bond between your unit is more than just friends. It's more than brothers even. And to leave one out or to separate in any way, I think would be devastating on many fronts."

"Still, I don't know that any of us have a clue what to do."

"You don't have to do anything. Technically you have homes to live in and pensions to pay your bills. You can just rest, and continue the spiritual and emotional healing that you've been doing. The mystery of Mouse was resolved. That closure and the additional passage of time is huge in and of itself."

"I know," he said. "Something that drove me for so long has ended. This first week afterward, I felt like I was staring at walls, not quite sure what to do with myself."

"And it may stay that way for another few weeks," she

said. "A transition period for you. And that's not a bad thing."

"I know, but I want to do something more ... worthwhile."

"So you want to go to the veteran hospitals and drag out patients for me? Future hires for you?"

He turned to look at her. "What do you mean?"

"A lot of men can't do even a fraction of what you do. Or what any of you do. Why not start some kind of retraining program? Physical, mental, emotional, whatever it is you feel you can do to help your own people."

"Help my own people," he said for emphasis.

She chuckled. "I mean military. Navy, air force, marines, army. However you feel you could help, do that to help them. Start a mentorship program."

He shook his head. "You know? We could do that on a volunteer basis, but it's not like we'll do that on a full-time basis. We have to have money incoming to keep everything flowing."

"So set up a business and bring on more people to train other former military people for something. Start something like what Levi has done, as we've discussed before. I still think that's a great idea. Levi started his business with just the four of them. Now how many does he employ?"

"Fifteen, sixteen, maybe twenty." Badger shook his head. "No idea. By the way, he called to say he and Ice were coming into town in a bit."

"Good. Will they stop by?"

"There was talk of it."

"It would be lovely to see them."

"The house is big enough, if you are okay for them to stay here. I mentioned it," he said, "but I had to check with you first."

She looked at him. "They are your friends."

He smiled. "But you live here too."

"And thank you very much for thinking of me," she said gently. "I'd love to see them."

He nodded. "Then I'll tell Levi. He didn't really have a set date. He said it could be next week or it could be in a couple months." He leaned over. "I'm thinking that he might be ready to ask Ice to marry him."

Kat stopped and stared at him for a long moment. "That would probably be a very good idea."

He frowned at her. "Why?"

"They've been together a long time," she said quietly. "I think Ice would like that."

"But she knows he loves her."

Her lips twitched. "Yes, and marriage isn't for everyone," she admitted. "But I think, inside, Ice would love to get married."

Badger nodded, but he was frowning too.

She chuckled and patted his hand. "I'll go grab the take-out menus."

"You want to grab me a beer while you're up?"

"Will do." She walked inside, straight through to the living room, where she knew he couldn't hear her and laughed. And laughed and laughed. Good for Ice. She was putting the first play in motion. Kat knew that she was taking a hell of a chance doing this, but she figured there really wasn't any other way. She'd need their support. All of them.

It was supposed to be a fun, happy event. But she definitely needed help. She'd been cajoling Stone to give them a hand, but he'd been less than amiable as it would put him in a difficult position himself. The thought just made her chuckle again. She picked up the take-out menus, grabbed a cold beer from the fridge and looked inside, thinking, *What the hell?* and pulled one out for her too. Outside she gave him a beer and sat down, still a big smile on her face.

"There you go again. You're making me suspicious," he growled.

She turned to look at him. "And what's bugging you now?"

He stared at her intently. "My intuition is going off on a full-tilt fire alarm."

"Yeah? Why?"

"I want to know what you're up to."

With a twinkle in her eyes, she leaned closer. "Maybe we should take the Chinese to bed."

His eyes lit up. "Now that's an idea I can get behind." And he started to get up.

She placed a hand on his thigh. "We haven't even ordered it yet."

He frowned as if trying to figure out the logistics.

She shook her head. "No way are we having sex, and then I have to get dressed to come downstairs, pay for the Chinese food and take it back upstairs again. I'll order it, and we'll eat first. That will give us a time frame." She motioned at the beer in his hand. "Besides, you haven't even had a drink yet."

He tilted the bottle back and downed almost half of it in one gulp.

At that, she burst out laughing. "What's the matter? A big strong man like you can't wait that long?"

He glared at her. "I waited two years to find you," he said. "Like hell we can't make good use of the ten-minute

14

delivery time, so place that order. Then we're going in the pool and ..." He wiggled his eyebrows suggestively.

She smirked, picked up the flyer, grabbed her phone and placed an order. Then she stood, tossed off her T-shirt, dropped her shorts, exposing the bathing suit she had on underneath. She looked at him with a big smile as she unclipped her leg, dropped it on the lounger, took one hop and fell into the water.

"Hey, that's cheating. I didn't even know you had a bathing suit on."

She broke through the water, laughing. "What difference would it have made?"

"I would have had you in there earlier if I'd known," he groaned. But he followed her into the pool within seconds.

She waited until he reached her, and then she slid her arms around his neck. "Our Chinese food will be at least thirty minutes."

He grinned, pulling her up tight. "That should give us lots of time."

"Yeah? Time for what?"

He slid his hands down her back to cup her cheeks and press her up tight against the hard ridge of his erection. "For anything you want."

She slowly slid her thighs up around his hips and wrapped her arms around his neck and smiled. "I was always into water sports."

"Thank God," he whispered fervently. And then he slid his hands up to her hair, holding her close, and kissed her.

The kiss was so much like everything she'd experienced since the nightmare of Mouse had come to an end. There was a freedom in his kiss, now that the fervent panic was gone, where they had to make every moment count because there might not be another one. Instead, now there was just that sense of their joy in coming together in peace and harmony and love. Like he'd said, she could get behind that.

She tightened her hold on him and hugged him and kissed him back with all the passion she felt.

THE NEXT MORNING Badger and Kat sat at the kitchen table, both drinking their coffee. Kat worked on her laptop, a big bright grin on her face, but then it fell away.

Badger was once again struck by Kat's actions. He studied her for a long moment.

She glanced at him, her smile back.

"Still not ready to tell me, huh?"

Her eyes went wide and innocent.

He sighed. "You wouldn't be trying to pull a surprise party or something on me, would you?" He glared at her in mock ire. "Because that's, like, not cool."

She sat back and chuckled. "What kind of surprise party would I throw? We have the guys over here every damn weekend as it is."

Maybe it was her swearing about the issue. Maybe it was a diversionary tactic. But he let himself be persuaded into the new topic. He leaned forward, crossed his arms on the table, his big hand wrapped around his mug. "It's not a problem for you? We never really talked about it." This time her smile and look of astonishment was real, and he knew enough about her to see that honesty.

It took her a moment to find the words. "You mean, the guys coming over every weekend?"

He nodded. He really wanted her to be okay with it. He

wanted everyone to be okay with it. Because these guys were his brothers. And he'd hoped that somehow, somewhere along the line, the women would become like sisters as well. But that was asking a lot. They didn't have the same bonding by fire that he and his unit had experienced over the years.

The women didn't have the same history, the same level of traumas. And, for that, he was grateful. He'd never want that for anybody. Yet it was almost too much to ask that seven unique women with various careers come together in the same unified front as the men in his unit had done. He knew every one of the women would do so out of respect for the strong bond between the men, and the women wanted their partners to be happy. Badger knew it would take more time for the women to come together in any kind of similar fashion. He just wanted that to happen now. He wanted to know in his heart of hearts it was all good.

She smiled, reached across and picked up his hand, stroking her thumb across his. "I love the guys. I think having everyone come on the weekend, like we do, as if Sundays are our time together as a group, as a family unit, is amazing. I think what you guys have achieved as friends is an incredible feat. And I don't think you realize how special it is."

He shrugged, feeling self-conscious. He knew how special it was, but he hadn't thought she did.

She chuckled. "And, yes, you should take a lot of the credit for that."

He shook his head. "No credit is due to me. It took all seven of us."

"Of course it did. At the same time, it also took your efforts to understand and to love each and every one of them as they are. And so you should be proud of what you've accomplished."

"I am. That doesn't mean I'm not a little worried about all the women's participation."

Her head tilted to the side, she studied him. "*Participation?*"

Uncomfortable now, he sat back, almost groaning silently.

But she knew him too well. She leaned forward. "*Participation?*"

"So maybe it's not the right word. I'd hoped ..." He had a hard time choosing his words. "I'd hoped that the seven of you would come to be as close as the seven of us are."

"Oh." She sat back, a smile playing around the corner of her lips. "You know? I think what we have is the grounds for a wonderful friendship between all of us. But it will take time. We're all very different. We've all come from very different backgrounds. We were thrown together for one common cause—Mouse."

"Just like me and the guys getting back together," Badger said with a quick nod. "Just like us."

"Exactly." Her grin got wider. "But the common issue, Mouse, has been resolved. And the women didn't have the years of training, of working together, that past which you men share. We didn't have all those years where you were forced to accept and deal with each other's weaknesses and strengths."

He frowned. "I know. And there's nothing I can really do about that."

"No, there's nothing you should try to do about it. You can't force a friendship. And I don't see that there's anything wrong with what we have. It will develop stronger and become easier over time."

He thrummed the table with his fingers. "And if I said I want it now?"

Her grin turned to laughter. "Just because you say so, doesn't make it so. Remember?"

He groaned. "I know it's foolish. But ..."

"But?" And then she got up, grabbed the coffeepot, returned to the table and refilled their cups. "You're afraid."

"I am not," he said in astonishment. But damn her smile was so gentle, so soft and so understanding that he could feel everything defensive inside him melting. She always had that effect on him.

"Yes, you are. You're afraid, if the women can't pull together like the men have, that we will end up being what breaks you all up."

He frowned. "I wouldn't have said that."

She chuckled. "No, you wouldn't. So I said it for you."

"Yeah, but, now that you've said it, I have to consider that possibility. And I don't like it," he announced.

She sat back down again with a tin of cookies in her hands.

He opened them and smiled. "Morning left these for us, didn't she?" He reached in eagerly. "Damn Geir for finding a cook like Morning." Immediately he looked up. "But I wouldn't trade her for you," he said hurriedly. At the knowing look in her eyes, he settled back. "Okay, so I might be a little nervous that everything is going so well right now. Nobody's shooting at us. Nobody's trying to kill us. Nobody's attacking our friends and family ..."

"You're getting bored, so you needed a problem to solve," she said in understanding. "Which is why I'd love to see you set up a business."

"We're talking about it, but we haven't really gotten any further than that. We're still recuperating."

She nodded. "Indeed. Yet there are seven of you. Very capable, very strong men, who are bored to tears."

He shrugged. "Not necessarily," he said cagily. "We're knocking around ideas."

"Good. Glad to hear that." She glanced at the clock. "I have to leave for work soon."

"Okay, the guys might be coming over in a bit, if that's okay?" He glanced at her wearily.

She stopped and studied him for a moment, then nodded. "Of course it's okay. It's your home."

"It's *our* home," he corrected.

"Any plans while they're here?"

Badger shook his head. "No. I think just more discussion about our futures and job options."

"Good. I'll see you later today." She stood, took her coffee cup to the kitchen sink, walked past him and snagged her purse. "Remember, I love you." She leaned over and kissed him gently on his temple. Dropped to give Dotty, always at Badger's side, a quick pat, and just like that she was gone.

He stared after her. He knew she was up to something. He just didn't know what.

She hadn't been gone ten minutes when a knock came at the front door. Dotty raced in front of Badger, barking, her tail wagging like crazy. He opened it to Cade and the others. He raised an eyebrow. "You just missed her."

"No, we were waiting for her to leave," Cade said with a grin. "Nothing like a little guy time."

"And you still made me get up and come to the door instead of letting yourself in?" growled Badger as he led the way back to the kitchen.

The guys spread out, some heading for the coffeepot, the others getting out cups.

"Of course. Otherwise you'll get lazy and sit too much. You know the doctor said you have to get up, move around for your leg's sake."

"Damn doctors." Badger flung himself onto the chair. "So what are we doing?"

"Well, we've tossed around a bunch of ideas, but the bottom line is, we need to start with something, then tweak it as we move forward."

Badger perked up. "Tell me more."

CHAPTER 2

K AT WALKED INTO her office, dropped her purse and headed straight for the coffeepot. Her assistant wasn't in yet. She frowned. It wasn't like him to be late. But she could hear his whistling as he came up the stairs now. She smiled as he walked through the door.

He raised his eyebrows and said, "You're not usually this early."

She glanced at her watch and shrugged. "It's not *that* early."

He chuckled. "Head on into your office. I'll get the coffee on."

She still had a good forty minutes before her first patient. Seated at her desk, she picked up the phone and called Honey.

"Kat, this is early for you," Honey said. "Are you in your office?"

"I just got in. I was thinking of something. I know it's probably very audacious, and it'll only work if you all back me on this. And it probably won't appeal to many in the group, so I'm looking for a saner head to tell me how this is a stupid idea."

"What's that?" Honey asked, her voice curious.

But then Honey was always up for something new and different. Which reminded Kat of Badger's conversation this morning—about him wanting the women to be best friends. She and Honey had already been friends for years, but they were definitely closer now.

"I was thinking about a surprise wedding," Kat said in a rush. She kept her voice low so her assistant, Jim, wouldn't hear.

"A surprise wedding," Honey said as if trying on the words. "You mean, you and Badger?"

"Yeah," she said hesitantly. "As in, he comes outside one day when all the guys are there, and there's a minister."

"Oh, wow." Then Honey didn't say anything more.

Kat winced, and her stomach sagged. "It's a shitty idea, isn't it?"

"No," Honey said cautiously. "You guys are great together. But how does Badger feel about surprises?"

"He doesn't like them." She stared moodily out her window. "I don't know why, but I just can't get this idea out of my head."

"Well, you could ask him to marry you first."

"I could, or he could ask me," she snapped, then groaned. "Shit."

Honey chuckled. "Why so impatient?"

"I don't know," Kat said. "But I have a feeling these men won't take that step easily. I mean, look at Ice and Levi. How many years have they been together, and they aren't married yet? But it's more than that with our guys. Something in these injured military men's psyches say they're broken, not deserving of a full and happy long-term future. Like they found us, and they should be damn grateful they've got us, but ..."

"But they're afraid to rock the boat in case we think this is short-term and how a more permanent outlook on our relationships could send any of us running away."

"Right. See? I knew you'd understand," Kat said. She could feel the relief washing through her. She started to pace her office. "I know it's kind of pushy, and I know it could possibly end badly, but I would really hope not. I've been talking to Ice about it, and she likes the idea."

"I guess the real question you have to ask yourself is," Honey said cautiously, "why now? Why the panic?"

"I'm not sure it's a panic. I'm not sure it is a rush. But I feel like the guys are dragging their heels on coming up with jobs, and that's okay. I'm not saying they have to get jobs or anything. They're all financially stable because of their pensions as it is. But I know they're bored, and I think bored men are dangerous."

"Well, a lot of renovation projects are going on because of their boredom," Honey said. "And we're still trying to get Geir a house on the block, at least within walking distance. So definitely some change is happening."

"I know. I know," Kat said. She thought for a moment. "I can't really explain it."

"Let me think about it," Honey said. "I'll get back to you. I've got a crazy-busy day ahead of me today. And obviously there's no need to settle anything this weekend." After a moment of silence she said, "Right?"

Kat chuckled. "No, no. I'm not talking about this weekend or even this month. I'm thinking I'll need a couple months to get ready."

"Right," Honey said with relief. "I was afraid you were really being crazy and jumping on this. I think, if you set it up properly, it'd be perfect. And would certainly make Badger decide one way or the other."

"Yeah, but you see? I don't want to lose him. I don't

want him to decide the wrong way," Kat said quietly.

"Let me think about it. And, no, don't expect me to call you back later today or tomorrow even. Give me a chance to roll this around in my head. We'll talk in a couple days, okay?"

Kat grinned. "Okay. I figured, if I could at least talk to you, you could keep me on the straight and narrow."

"Knowing you for a decade or more now, I don't remember ever hearing you mention anything along this line at all. I didn't think you were into surprise parties even."

"I know. It's not me. Yet, at the same time, I feel like this is what it'll take to get Badger to take the step."

"Maybe he's not ready. Did you consider that?"

"I know he isn't. But I don't think he ever will be because I think he would feel he'd be a noose around my neck. As long as everything's good, he'll keep living as he is. But, if his health declines, no way will he marry me."

"Right." Honey gave a heavy sigh. "I think that could probably be said for all of them."

"Exactly. And I don't want to take that chance."

"Give me a couple days. I've got to run." And Honey hung up.

Kat put the phone down on her desk.

Just then Jim walked in and placed a cup of coffee in front of her and her daily appointment sheet. "So, once again, it appears you've overbooked yourself."

"Isn't that why you took over the booking?" she joked.

"If you would stop answering the phone and sneaking in appointments where there is no room for them ..."

She groaned. "Okay, give it to me straight. How bad is it?"

"Bad," he said cheerfully. "We'll have to be extremely

efficient to get through this."

"That could be rough."

"It'll definitely be rough, but we can do it." He turned to walk back to the door. "But you have to follow my timing. Got it?"

At that, she nodded. "Got it." And she took one look at the schedule he'd placed in front of her and groaned again. "Why do I always do this?"

"Because you care too much," came his answer.

"Dammit." He was right. She did care too much. It was really hard for her to say no to anyone. That was just the facts of life.

He buzzed her phone a few minutes later. "This is a good start to the day. Your first appointment came in ten minutes early. If you can get him out five minutes ahead of schedule, you'll have eased up fifteen minutes."

She bowed her head for a moment and then said, "Send him in." Just as the door opened, she put on a bright smile and thought to herself, *You did this. Buck up and handle it.* "Hi," she said as her patient walked in.

"WE STILL HAVEN'T figured out exactly what it is we want to do. So far, all we've done is renovate our houses and adapt to our partners' needs. Laszlo, we have to complete that home office for Minx. And, Geir, you need a home studio for Morning, right?"

Geir spoke up. "Yes. We discussed it over the weekend. She really can't work within a small space. And it has to have proper ventilation."

"Since you're renting, you need a bigger house," Erick

said.

Geir nodded. "But nothing is even available in this area by Badger's house anymore."

Badger said, "We could talk to the neighbors and see if anybody wants to sell."

"But we'd have to pay a premium that way," Geir said. "That'll be an issue."

"It always is," Badger said with a nod. "Unless we all relocate." He glanced around his home. "I'd hate to …"

"You're the only one who is really attached to their home. But you have a very good reason for it," Talon said. "None of us want to see you lose that."

"Sure, but if we all want to be within walking distance, then we have to do something."

"It might just take some time," Geir said. "If I could find something right now that would allow Morning a proper space to work in, I'd grab it. … I don't want her to feel creatively cramped."

"I know that upcoming showing of hers is very important. Her development is just as important as the rest of ours."

"There are a couple of lots in this neighborhood, if we're into building new homes," Jager said.

"True enough, and Allison doesn't have any major hobbies that she needs extra space for," Badger said.

Jager nodded. "Our house is just a house, nothing special about it. But I've lived in worse."

They all knew it wasn't about the house; it was about who lived in it that mattered.

"Even if I could find what Morning and I wanted, and I had to drive or bike over, it wouldn't matter to me," Geir said. "It's all about getting Morning some space and quick.

She's got her upcoming show to paint for. She's pretty worried about it too."

"Anybody here have a real estate agent they know or trust?"

Erick shook his head. "No. Not me."

Cade shook his head too. Badger turned his gaze on Talon and Laszlo. They both shook their heads. Back over to Geir and then Jager.

"I think Dennis's wife is in real estate," Jager said quietly.

Instantly they froze. "Is she?"

Jager shrugged. "I can ask." He pulled out his phone and quickly brought up his contact info for Allison's brother, who worked for the police department in Santa Fe. "I'm sending a text now." His fingers clicked on his phone. When he hit Send, he looked up and said, "I believe Allison said something about it."

"If so, Dennis's wife could be a big help to us right now."

"She might, but she could also be very busy," Jager said with a grin. "Three kids, remember?"

The men nodded thoughtfully.

When Jager's phone went off a few minutes later, still sitting in Jager's hands, he looked down and said, "Yes, she is a Realtor. Dennis is asking if I want her to call us."

"Yes," Geir said. "Let's bring her onboard so we can get her opinion."

"The market's a little crazy right now," Erick said.

"It's actually fairly stable," Cade stated. "It's starting to climb, but it's still a good time to buy. Once it goes really crazy, you can end up paying so much more just because the market will tolerate that higher pricing."

"I'll have her call me," Jager said. "Then I'll pass Geir's name on to her. If that's okay, Geir?"

"That's the best way to do it. I'm thinking about what Morning and I need, but what's really important is a studio for her."

"She can always take over the living room," Badger joked. "You know any one of us would do it, if it was important to our partners."

Geir nodded. "And I wouldn't mind. But Morning would. She had a huge house in California with a huge added-on studio."

"I don't know that you can find anything that size in this subdivision," Erick said.

"We don't need that total size," Geir said. "She's not planning on running a B and B anymore."

"Has the sale of that gone through yet?"

Geir nodded. "Not quite. A few more days before it closes. After they pay off the mortgage, and she splits the net money with her father, she'll have a really nice nest egg."

"You probably could buy a mansion here in Santa Fe for that bit of money," Badger said.

Geir shrugged. "She could. I can't say I've got a ton saved. I certainly haven't spent anything for the last couple years, but my savings doesn't equate to California real estate chunks."

"Right," Cade said. "She's lucky she managed to hang on to it as long as she did because the market certainly hasn't done them a disservice. I understand her father needed his asset base back, but, by waiting that much longer to get Morning a little more established, the real estate values have gone up more, and they both made a nice chunk of profit."

They all nodded.

"And what about our future business? Anybody come up with any ideas on what we want to do, or what you individually want to do?" Badger asked.

Just plain silence followed.

"See? That's where the problem is," Badger stated. "Kat says we still need to heal. But she says that bored men become a distraction and may get into the wrong things," he joked. "And I, for one, can't necessarily say I'm happy with nothing to do. We've had such a heavy focus in our lives, always a regimented lifestyle while in the service. Then, while healing, it was physiotherapy and medications and sleep and exercise and eating right. Then dealing with Mouse. Now we have the women." He shook his head. "And it's like, after all the hunting we did, everything has come to a stop. I don't know how to get started again."

"Honey would say we're looking in the wrong direction," Erick offered.

All the men turned to look at Erick.

He shrugged. "I can see what she means. We've already done everything we planned to do. We have to turn around and find something very new."

"But it's all we know," Cade said. "What the hell are we supposed to do now?"

"Allison first suggested we look at a training center to retrain men to do security work, like Levi's company does," Badger reminded them. "Kat was just talking this morning about helping men like us get back into the real world."

"But isn't that like counseling?" Talon asked. His voice held just enough horror in it for the others to start laughing.

Jager chuckled. "Well, I, for one, don't feel like I could counsel anyone. If it's more about training men to deal with getting back into the real world, maybe. But I think we're better off with a company where we can hire people with various skills or at least train them in those skills and give them viable jobs."

"And that brings us back around again to what company?" Badger asked.

"Exactly. And who the hell knows, right?" Erick said.

CHAPTER 3

TWO DAYS LATER Kat looked up from her lunch and stared out the window. She still hadn't heard from Honey. Kat knew it had been a lot to ask. Even now she was waffling on the idea herself. She didn't know why it appealed so much, but she figured she needed to trust her gut and to get a jump on it. She was incredibly good at figuring this planning stuff out. Maybe it was just fun keeping this a surprise from Badger. Maybe it was just that she wanted so much more. But she really wanted to see if she could pull off this surprise wedding.

Just then her personal phone rang. She pulled her cell toward her and smiled when she saw Honey's name. She answered it and left it on the desk, putting it on Speakerphone. "I was just thinking about you."

"All good things I hope." Honey laughed. "I have to admit that, since we talked a couple days ago, I haven't been able to think of much else."

"Is that a good thing or a bad thing?" Kat asked.

"I'll tell you what it is. It's a bad thing. Because, if you're doing that with Badger, maybe I want to do it with Erick."

Kat gasped, sat back, tossed down her pen and then started to laugh. "Can you imagine?"

"It's not that funny," Honey said crossly. "And I blame you for putting that idea in my mind."

"I know. But, once it's in there, it's almost impossible to take it out, isn't it?"

"And I brought up long-term with Erick a couple days ago—actually the same night I spoke to you—and he gave me the gentlest smile that said he wouldn't want to rock the boat. That everything was going along just fine as it was."

"Did you bring up marriage with him?" Kat asked, horrified.

Honey sighed. "No. Not at all. I was just looking at where he was going mentally with our future. Now I don't know if he thought I was talking about marriage, or maybe he thought I was talking about him and his future job. He seems to think he needs to do something more productive, or he is not the man of the house."

Kat chuckled. "Right. And how awkward is that? We women all have jobs or something lined up. But the guys don't have jobs."

"I know, but they're bringing in money on their own."

"Oh, I hear you, but I think it's their need to do something much more."

"And that won't be easy to find. They have to make that decision for themselves. So, anyway, I think what Erick was trying to say is, that he'd get there eventually."

"So you deliberately kept your discussion away from the relationship stuff?"

"Yes and no. But he wasn't coming up to snuff either way."

Kat chuckled. "No, I think the guys all have this idea that they're broken. They haven't seen just how much they've healed. So what do you think about the idea?"

"I don't know. I want to proceed, yet I'm scared as hell Erick will turn me down. That won't be a relationship fix for sure. And then I made another mistake—or maybe not a mistake. I don't know." Honey spoke so fast that she was running over her words.

Kat shook her head. "Honey, what are you talking about?"

"I might have mentioned it to Minx."

"Well, that's a surprise."

"Right? And the thing is, she started to laugh and said it would be perfect."

"Badger and me? Me marrying Badger would be perfect?" Kat asked, clarifying what was perfect.

"*And* me and Erick." In a rush Honey added, "And maybe her and Laszlo?"

Kat stared out the window in horrified shock. "What if we all did it?"

"That's the thing. I don't think it'll work unless all of us do it."

"I don't think we'll get all of us to do it in two months' time," Kat said.

"No, that would be asking a lot."

"But we don't know that for sure until we talk to them." Silence followed.

"I need to get back to work," Kat said, "and let this settle for a bit."

"How about we talk at this same time in two more days?" Honey said. "My next patient is here. Got to go."

Kat glanced at her schedule. She still had a good five minutes. And she would need it because this was just way too crazy to be believed. But, at the same time, her heart was jumping with joy.

For the rest of the afternoon she caught herself chuckling at odd moments. By the time she got home, she had a silly grin plastered on her face. She walked in, headed straight for Badger, who was sitting by the pool, his laptop open, papers all around him. She gave him a great big hug and dropped a kiss on his cheek.

"Wow, that's a nice greeting." He took one look at her face and narrowed his gaze. "We're back to that whole question of *What's going on with you?*"

She shrugged. "I had a good day." But in spite of trying to moderate her voice, it was too perky.

Badger's arched eyebrow and studious glare told her so.

She walked inside, putting away her purse and keys. Afterward she returned to the entryway, took off her coat and hung it up in the coat closet. Then she headed back to the kitchen. Instead of coffee, she walked toward the fridge and pulled out a beer. She peered around the corner to see Badger already working on a beer.

She joined him outside, sitting down beside him. "What's for dinner?"

He looked up and frowned. "I haven't gotten that far. I'm not a very good stay-at-home partner, am I?"

"I don't think we've brought up any rules on that, have we?" she asked in a half-joking manner. But she heard some tension in his voice. "I was thinking burgers." She nodded, liking the idea even more. "We have ground meat in the fridge. I could mix up some nice big patties with feta cheese and herbs in them."

"We just had burgers yesterday," he said cautiously.

"So? Does that mean we can't have burgers two days in a row?"

"Feta burgers would be awesome." His voice gained some enthusiasm. "I thought women didn't like to eat the same thing two days in a row."

She stared at him. "You do say the darnedest things."

He shrugged. "I'm okay to eat burgers every day of the week." He lifted his beer. "It's man's food."

She rolled her eyes. "I'll make a salad to go with them."

"Yeah, that's woman's food," he said with a big grin.

"Can you barbecue the burgers?" At his nod, she hopped to her feet. "I'm really hungry. I'll prep the patties." She dashed inside, pulled out the meat and herbs she wanted and the feta cheese from the fridge, and tossed it all into a bowl, combining it with her hands.

She deliberately didn't treat Badger as if he was disabled. She had her own problems, and he had his. She saw him get up, walk to the grill and light it. She smiled. He was a hell of a guy.

Why did she want to push the marriage issue? Fear that his health would worsen and he'd never marry her? *We all aren't getting any younger.* Fear that he'd leave her? He still could. It wasn't as if divorce wasn't an option down the road. Or maybe she was afraid he'd prefer to be more friends than committed partners. Not an easy thought. Still, if she knew they were together forever, why was she forcing the issue?

Because it wasn't enough. Still, she'd much rather surprise him completely. Either he'd make it or he'd break it, and she'd have the best day of her life, or it would be the worst.

"The barbecue is hot," he called to her.

"Burgers are ready," she called back. She formed them and laid them on a plate. She made six. She carried the plate out to the grill and handed it to him. "I figure I could take one with the salad for my lunch at work tomorrow. You'll eat two tonight and have two more to reheat for your lunch tomorrow. As long as you're okay eating burgers three days in a row," she teased.

He chuckled. "I like my food any way I can get it."

"Me too." They both stood by the grill until she remembered she hadn't made the salad. "Oops," she said, racing inside. There she chopped lettuce, cucumbers, tomatoes, tossed it all with salad dressing and carried the salad bowl out with their dinner plates and two more beers on a serving tray. "Do you want to eat at the table or on our lounges?"

"Lounges," he said. "Do we have any chips left?"

"No idea." She set up their tableware and popped open their beers. When she turned around, she saw him moving into the kitchen, rummaging for the leftovers from the previous days' barbecues. "What are you working on with your laptop?" she asked as she put a small end table between them, so they could reach the salad and condiments without any trouble.

"Just paperwork," he said. "Talked to a real estate agent today."

She froze. "You did?" She barely concealed the horror in her voice as she stared at him "You're not thinking about selling your house, are you?"

He looked at her for a moment. "Would that bother you?"

She dropped her gaze. How did she answer that? "First of all, I'm not with you because of your house. But I know how much this place means to you. And I have to admit that I've fallen in love with it too."

He reached out a hand and gently stroked the hair off her face. "I don't think you're here because of my house," he said for clarification. "And it's not me looking to sell or buy. Geir doesn't own a house, and we're trying to find him one that's got a studio for Morning."

"Right," she said, "but those look like floor plans."

He nodded. "There is a vacant one-acre lot on the next block over."

"I remember that one. Could you build him a house?"

He shrugged. "I could. It depends on the money though."

"But Morning has a nice chunk coming from the sale of the B and B, doesn't she?"

"Sure, but not everybody is ready to build."

As she studied him, she looked closer at the plans. "Are these your plans?"

"I always thought I'd build a house someday because I wasn't expecting my parents to die as soon as they did. At least twenty years too early."

She nodded. "You would've had fun with that, wouldn't you?"

"I like working with my hands."

"What about the other guys? Are they any good at it?"

"Jager is hell on wheels as an electrician. But he's not certified for residential wiring. He might have to upgrade or something. I'm not sure. And does he even want to?"

"Exactly. Lots of issues to consider." She studied him for a moment and frowned. "Does he really know what he's doing?"

Badger nodded. "He does. He also knows another guy who is a licensed electrician amongst other things."

"So?"

He glanced at her and shrugged. "I don't know. Everything is up in the air."

"Who's this licensed guy?"

"A veteran," he said shortly. "He did his training in the military, got his license when he came out."

"Oh, I like that idea," she said.

"Why?"

"I think anytime you use the ex-servicemen and their newly repurposed skills, it's a good thing."

"I don't know how much newly retrained he is. But he is certainly licensed."

"Is he superbusy? Would he have time to help?"

Badger plunged his hands into his pockets and just stared at the barbecue grill.

She wondered what was going on.

After a moment he said, "You might have seen him."

She stopped and looked at him. "I might have?"

"In your practice. Yeah. He's missing his lower left leg."

She stared at him for a moment. "Ethan?"

Badger gave her a lopsided grin. "Yeah, Ethan."

"He's not working at all, is he?"

"No, he's had a setback but he is trained, and he is qualified. But I'd have to spead with him. He's got some stuff going on in his life too."

"And so you want to put him to work? Help him to heal?" she asked, finally understanding where he was coming from. "I think it's a great idea."

Badger shrugged. "We're not sure what the hell we're doing yet. It's only an idea we're discussing at the moment. Among others."

"You find any carpenters in the former vet club?"

"Maybe. One guy was a framer until he fell. He did five years in the navy and then went back to civilian life but had a bad accident while he was working on a building."

"And he's injured?"

"Injured enough that he doesn't feel he can go back to work full-time as a framer."

"How about working part-time with you guys?"

"It'll be just the one job," Badger said in a cautionary voice.

"Sure, it would," she said with a big grin. "Is Erick looking to build too?"

"Hard to say. None of us really knows what the hell we're doing."

"What about helping out Levi?"

"As you know, that's been discussed too."

But he didn't say anything more, and she didn't want to push him. Like her, they were all feeling their way. "Let's eat."

BADGER WONDERED IF he should tell her that he'd seen somebody on the property today. He also thought he had heard a knock on the door when he was out by the pool. By the time he'd gotten there, nobody was outside. He hadn't been suspicious until he walked in the kitchen and thought he saw somebody walking around the house. Dotty raced to the glass doors barking. When he stepped outside, a woman looked at him then at the dog nervously.

"Oh! I was just taking measurements."

He frowned at her.

"A woman named Kat requested it," she said nervously. "I did knock on the door to see if anybody was home."

He nodded. "I was in the pool but got out when I thought I heard the dog barking."

She picked up her bag and said, "I'll come back later." And she bolted to the side of the house.

He'd stood there for a long time, then wandered off to

the side of the pool, where she'd been standing before a large grassy piece of the backyard. It was one of the prettiest spots because of all the roses he had planted along the back of the property. Roses had been his mother's favorite flower. As he'd stood there and stared at the house, he just didn't get it. What the hell could anybody possibly be measuring out here for? And what did Kat have to do with it?

But he hadn't asked her. And now he didn't know if he could because, if she was up to something, he didn't want to spoil the surprise. At the same time, it was a little disturbing to think she was measuring for something around his house.

And then he winced. See? That was the problem. He was still thinking of it as *his* house. *His* place. And yet truly, while she lived here, it was theirs. She had her own house, but, if he wanted to keep her here with him, he had to start thinking of *his* house as being *their* house. So he would just sit back and relax and let her say something to him on her own. "Anything interesting happen today?" he asked as he picked up some chips.

She shook her head. "Nope. Talked to Honey once. Just a busy day."

"How is Honey?"

She slid him a look. "She's fine."

"Is everybody still coming this weekend?"

She stopped with a chip in midair. "I forgot to ask."

"What did you talk about then?"

"It was just a touching-base kind of a call," she said carefully, and then she picked up her burger and took a big bite, effectively cutting off the conversation.

He thought about all the holidays coming up in the second half of the year. He wanted her to feel comfortable enough to do whatever she was planning, but it was unnerving. He wasn't big on surprises. Especially not surprise parties. "So are you happy in this house? Is there anything you would want to change?"

Startled, she glanced at him, but her mouth was full of food. She had to chew and swallow first. "I wouldn't change anything," she said, astounded. "It's fantastic just as it is."

CHAPTER 4

T HE NEXT DAY Kat got a phone call from the wedding planner she'd consulted.

"I might have blown it," Marisa announced.

"What are you talking about?" Kat asked.

"I was looking on Google Maps, so I didn't have to go to the house, trying to get a good idea of the size and space, but couldn't get a close-enough look," she said, her normal enthusiasm waning. "So I figured, if I made a quick visit to the house, I could tell if we had enough room or not."

Kat gasped and sank back against her chair. "Oh, no," she moaned.

"Yeah. I did knock on the door yesterday, but there was no answer, so I figured it would be safe. I ran around to the back and took some measurements. But, just when I was done, he stepped onto the back porch. And I might have said I was there at your request." Her words came out in a rush.

Kat pinched the bridge of her nose. "Oh, my God."

"I'm sorry," Marisa said. "I'm so sorry."

"Oh, my God." Kat didn't know what else to say or think. "Well, that explains his cryptic comments last night about if I wanted to change anything about the house."

"He said that?" Marisa asked in amazement. "He didn't ask you what I was doing there?"

"No, he's waiting to see if I come forward and say something first."

"I was only there for a few minutes," she murmured.

Kat groaned and stared out the window. "Let me think about how to handle this."

"Okay. There is one good thing though," Marisa added.

"Yeah, what's that?"

"You have lots of room," and she quickly hung up the phone.

"What difference does it make if there's a lot of room in the backyard if he's now so suspicious I can't even do this?" Kat muttered out loud.

Her assistant popped his head around the door. "Did you say something?"

She shook her head. "Nope. Just talking to myself."

"That doesn't sound good." He stared at her for a moment. "You seem to be really preoccupied these days."

She nodded. "Yeah, I was just thinking about doing something sneaky, but I might have been caught already." She shook her head, got up and walked to the window. "Serves me right for trying to plan a surprise."

"Hey, planning surprise parties takes real talent."

That got a chuckle out of her. "Are you saying I can't do it because I have no talent for it?"

"No, no, no, no, that's not what I meant," he cried out. "But I do have a talent for that stuff," he said proudly. "I pull off those kinds of parties all the time."

"Yeah? How about a surprise wedding?" she asked starkly. "Think you can pull that off?"

He stared at her, a bit of confusion on his face. "Whose wedding?"

She glared at him.

And then he got it. "Oh my gosh. You want to surprise

Badger with a wedding?" Instantly Jim stepped backward. He frowned and put his hands on his hips. "I'm not sure that's a good idea."

"I'm not either," she said, fatigue in her voice. "But it's the cards I'm dealing with right now."

"Well, you could be very modern. Ask him to marry you."

"I was thinking about it," she said, staring out the window, watching the cars go back and forth. "And then I thought, with somebody like him, I probably shouldn't give him time to think about it. It should be fait accompli. He should come home one day, with a reason to be in a suit. Hell, I don't give a shit if he wears a suit or not, but he probably will. And I'll be out in the garden, waiting for him."

"But the men are supposed to be in the garden waiting for the bride."

She chuckled. "Yeah, I haven't figured that one out yet."

Jim stepped up and looked out the window with her. "I'd love to be part of it."

She slipped him a sideways glance. "Part of what?"

"The whole thing," he said enthusiastically. "Oh, my God, it would be such a rush."

She glared at him. "Unless Badger is upset and doesn't like a pincher move like that."

"You know something? He would really like it."

"How do you figure?"

"Because he poses those kinds of moves all the time. So, if he got caught in one himself, he would think you outsmarted him. And *that* he would appreciate."

"But I don't want him tricked into it," she said. "I want him to marry me because he loves me."

"You won't *trick* Badger into anything. He won't marry you to save face. If anything, you're taking a huge chance putting Badger on the spot like that. Because he could say no."

She nodded. "I know. I know that all too well."

"Do you have anybody to help you?"

She shrugged. "I was talking to Honey. She can't stop thinking of joining me by setting up Erick too."

At hearing a strangled sound from Jim, Kat turned to look at him. Found an odd look on his face. "What?"

"Well, there's no way in hell you can do two surprise weddings, if you think about it. There are seven of you. Seven brides for seven men," and he started to rub his hands. "Oh, my God."

She shook her head. "No way. No way we can pull it off times seven."

"But you have to," he said. "Because, if one couple isn't involved, that man will feel unloved. That what they have isn't as strong as what the rest of you have. That would be devastating to him. So, if only one of you does this, you could get away with it, maybe. Maybe because you and Badger were the first to couple up in this group. But that's the only pass you get. After that, it has to be all seven together, so no one feels left out." And he started to pace her office. "You need a reason for the celebration. You need a reason for the men to have suits on. You need a reason to get them all at your place."

"Well, that's easy enough. They come every Sunday."

He nodded. "Right. So this time we just have to have a way to make it fancier."

"What do you suggest?"

He turned to her. "I'm not sure. We need to think on

this. It's got to be a compelling reason for them to come, all dressed up."

She nodded. "Ice is willing to help out. Though I'm not too sure what help to ask her for." She added humorously, "I talked to Stone to see if he'd give me a hand, and he was horrified at the whole thing and said hell no."

Her assistant chuckled. "He's got a girlfriend of his own, doesn't he?"

She grinned. "That's the thing. No matter who we get to help, they're all in the same boat. If they help us, their girlfriends or boyfriends will look at what we're doing here and start thinking about their own situations."

Just then her phone rang. She pulled it out to find a call from Ice. She hit the Talk button and waved Jim back out to the front room. "Hi, Ice. What's up?"

"I can rope Levi into this," Ice said. "Matter of fact, we talked about it. I explained a little bit about what you wanted to do."

"Was he horrified?" Kat asked in a dry tone. "Because Stone sure as hell was."

Ice chuckled. "Actually Stone's quite intrigued by the whole idea. After you contacted him, he's done a lot of thinking about what he could do to help. The three of us have been talking. We could make it an engagement party. Levi would set it up so your guys would all know he's going to ask me to marry him. Of course our guys won't know. Stone is making sure he and I and Levi do our talking in the control room only when it's just us around."

Kat listened in astonishment as Ice laid out the plan. "Oh, my God."

"Is it too much?" Ice asked, her tone laced with humor. "It was Levi's idea. I was quite surprised he came up with it.

Of course it's just a cover," she added hurriedly.

"Well, it's an incredibly romantic one. And I'd love to host your engagement party—even as a cover," Kat said with a laugh. "It would certainly be a reason for the guys to dress up."

"Yeah, but," Ice said, "the engagement party ruse is just for the guys to know. You can't know about that. You'll need your own ruse on your end for having a more formal affair."

"I'll have to give it some thought." Her mind raced as she thought about it. "There'd be a lot of organizing to do."

"Yep, sure would be," Ice said. "I could probably get some help from here, if you don't have anyone in mind."

"The question really is, how many?"

"How many what?"

Kat brought up her latest conversation with Honey.

As soon as Ice heard the whole thing, she started to laugh. "Oh, my God. This is too priceless. But that would be perfect. Levi can contact the guys, tell them what he's planning. Tell them he wants it formal. Maybe Labor Day weekend. We were planning on coming that weekend anyway."

Kat slapped a hand over her mouth as she thought about it. She didn't know what to say. But it was an incredibly ballsy idea. "Do you think the guys will hate it?" she asked fearfully.

"Badger? It's likely the only way you'll get that coot up to the altar," Ice said, chuckling. "Do I think he'd hate you for it? No, absolutely not. It's a sign of how much you care. Anyway, like I said, I've just had a casual conversation with Levi about it, nothing for sure and nothing set in stone. So think about it, talk to the others, see what you want to do, and then get back to me." Just before she hung up, she said, "And, yes, it takes a lot of balls to do something like this. And I'm damn sorry I didn't think of it myself." And then laughing again, she hung up.

It was funny because Kat never really thought about how Ice and Levi weren't legally married. Because they seemed already married. It was obvious they were 100 percent devoted to each other, but they weren't even engaged. It wasn't Levi's style to make a big deal out of marriage, although he might do it for Ice's sake.

Kat turned to stare at her desk when Jim popped his head around the corner. "So, what was that?" he asked in excitement. "I thought I heard something about the wedding."

She smiled. "Well, this is what Ice just suggested." And she quickly explained it.

His face lit up, and he almost danced in place. "That would be perfect. I mean, why not make a big party out of it?"

"But why not have the party at Levi's home? There's got to be thirty of his team members living at the compound in Houston, plus their significant others."

"Because maybe that's where the wedding will be. If he can do an engagement party with you guys, then he can have the wedding at home."

Kat said with a knowing smile, "It's because it is entirely fake that he can do this at all." Now that she understood how to make that work, she started to think this could actually be pulled off. "You know this just might work."

Jim grinned. "In that case, we have a ton of shit to take care of."

She shook her head. "No, we're not going anywhere

with this yet. Just because I might do this to Badger, that doesn't mean the other ladies want to."

"I highly suggest we find out, and we find out fast. It's the middle of July. You've got about six weeks to Labor Day weekend."

"Six weeks." She shook her head. "That's not very long."

"No, it's not, but it's long enough," he said. "The thing is, the Labor Day weekend is an incredibly popular weekend to get married, so you guys would also have to figure out who would marry you, and we'd have to book him fast."

She winced. She didn't even know what denomination everybody was. It would only take one who needed a strictly religious wedding to make this all not work out.

Her assistant said, "Honestly, the easiest would be a justice of the peace. Somebody who can come to the location, and we can have the wedding outside your house. Because that is one hell of a beautiful house and a gorgeous backyard."

"Sure," she said slowly. "But the justice of the peace would have to know he was coming to do seven weddings."

"It's actually one wedding ceremony. He just has to repeat a couple lines seven times." Jim was so thrilled he gripped his hands in prayer mode, staring at her, an eager beaver ready to jump on this job.

She held up a hand. "We still have to wait."

He nodded, sadness falling on his face. "You have to tell me soon though," he said, "because we must get on this and get on this fast."

"Let me talk to Honey." She sat back down at her desk, alone once again, and looked at her phone, then realized Honey was with patients all afternoon. So Kat sent her a text. **Contact me before you go home. I talked to Ice.**

And then she dialed the phone and contacted Minx.

"What's up, Kat?"

"You talked to Honey?"

Minx chuckled. "I did. And, since then, I haven't been able to think of anything else."

"Right? Me too. Not sure this is a good idea though."

"I think it'll be a blast. I think it's … perfect."

Kat sat back. "Why and how?"

"I've always made decisions fairly quickly. And I'm more than ready to jump forward in this new world and leave all that shit from my old world behind me. I've made a lot of changes in the last few months. But more needs to happen. And that suits me. I really like the idea," she said with a chuckle in her voice. "But I think we have to check with the other women too."

"I know. But it feels like we've got a conspiracy going on. Badger's already suspicious."

At that, Minx laughed out loud. "It'll be hard to keep it quiet with our seven intel-gathering ex-navy SEALs," she admitted. "So, the sooner, the better."

"Labor Day weekend?"

"What?" Minx said in excitement. "Is this really going to happen?"

"I heard from Ice today, and she had an interesting proposition." She quickly shared the news.

Before long, Minx was laughing her head off. "Oh, my God, that's perfect. That is *so* perfect."

"Do you think it's believable? Do you think the guys would follow through and believe this?"

"Well, if it came from Levi himself, they all would. Levi is a straight shooter."

"So true."

"I'll talk to Faith," Minx said. "She's flying back today. I'm supposed to meet her tomorrow for coffee as it is."

"Right. I miss that. I work Monday to Friday, and it's hard to get away during the week."

"That'll change. You'll have to clear your schedule somewhat now. We can't meet to plan this with the girls on the weekends, and we can't discuss it on our Sunday afternoon barbecues. Not if we want to keep this a surprise from our guys. So we'll have to meet for lunch and or take coffee breaks together in order to keep this all on track."

Minx hung up soon afterward and left Kat sitting here, staring at the phone. If Minx talked to Faith, then four of them would be involved. There were still three more.

Just then Jim popped in and said, "Your patient finally arrived."

Kat gave him a big smile. "Good. It'll give me something else to think about." And she set about working the rest of her afternoon.

BADGER STARED AT the house plans, while the other guys looked on over his shoulders.

"This is a great idea," Geir said. "Though I'm not sure Morning had a chance to look at it yet."

"She definitely needs to see these. Being a cook and an artist, she'll want a special kitchen and her big well-vented studio. Not sure how she'll feel about the rest of the house," Badger said with a laugh. "But there's time. None of us needs to rush into anything."

Geir grinned, then said abruptly, "Levi called me earlier today."

Badger and the other guys looked at Geir. "What's up?" Badger asked.

"He wanted to know if I could play bodyguard to somebody in Santa Fe at the capitol building. They're expecting trouble with a difficult decision coming down to a vote on the floor."

"So you'll show up as extra muscle?" Badger frowned at him. "Are you going to the Roundhouse alone?"

"He tried to contact you," Geir said. "But you didn't get back to him."

Badger pulled up his phone and swore when he saw the text. "I missed it. I feel like I'm off my game."

"Anything bothering you?" Geir asked.

"Kat. Something's going on with her, and I can't figure it out."

The men just looked at him.

He shrugged. "I don't think it's major, but something is niggling away at me." He knew the others would understand that. When something nagged him like that, it was damnnear impossible for him to let it go. It was usually something he needed to pay attention to.

"It could be a minor thing," Erick said.

"I know. It will be minor." And he felt much better having expressed that much of what disturbed him.

"Any idea what it's about?" Talon now sprawled on the living room couch in front of him.

Badger pointed at the backyard. "A woman was in the backyard with a tape measure."

Instantly the men perked up. "What?"

"Right?" Badger shrugged. "There was a knock on the door." He laughed. "Honestly I just came out of the pool, and I didn't have a whole lot of clothing on. I raced to the door, soaking wet, with my crutches. But no one was there. But by the time I returned to the backyard, a woman ran around the house. I stopped her, and she smiled and apologized, saying Kat had sent her to take some measurements, and then she skedaddled on me."

"What did Kat say?"

Badger shot them a look. "I didn't say anything to her."

The others stared at him for a long moment.

"Why not?" Talon asked.

Badger sighed. "Because I feel like she thinks this is my house, not our house. I want her to feel like it's her house too. I did ask her if she wanted to change anything about the house, and she sounded genuinely shocked and said she loved the place."

The men nodded as they stared around the living room.

"It's a great house." Erick was sincere.

Badger nodded. "So then what's the deal with the woman in the backyard with a tape measure?"

The men stared at each other and shrugged.

"No clue," Talon answered.

"When is your birthday? Maybe she's got a party planned for you? Maybe she's putting in an outdoor kitchen or something?"

The men warmed to the idea, each one coming up with more plans, better, over and above the other ideas.

Badger sat back with a smile on his face. That was the thing about good friends. They weren't immediately jumping to the wrong idea; they jumped to good and great ideas. "An outdoor kitchen would be a hell of a deal," he admitted.

"Would she do it without you being in on it?" Geir asked.

He shook his head. "No, I don't think she would get it done without me because she'd want my input. But she might be getting measurements to see what would work." Instantly he felt better because that was so like Kat. She was such a giving person, and he knew he could trust her. She would never put him on the spot over something. And that was one of the reasons he really loved her. Kat's acceptance was worth so much. He chuckled. "That makes a lot of sense. My birthday is in September. But, hey, it'll probably take a while to plan and build something like that."

"Yeah, a long time. Besides, maybe she wants a garden. Better than what you've got. Maybe she wants to put in more roses."

Badger glanced at the backyard where the woman had been. "That is a rose bed."

The men chuckled.

"Maybe she wants a wooden swing for two or a hammock? You never know."

After that, the men returned to the discussion about building houses. "I think we can keep renting for a while," Geir said. "Morning did mention that maybe she could rent a studio."

"How do you feel about that?"

Geir shook his head. "I'd like to keep her home honestly. At least that way I can keep an eye on her."

"Do you think she's still in danger here?"

"No, not at all," Geir said. He gave a sheepish grin. "I just like looking after her."

And, for the first time, Badger thought about that as he settled deeper into the couch, wondering if Kat wasn't right. All of them were men with protective instincts, coming from a lifestyle where their defensive skills were needed. And now they had nothing to defend. If they were bored, then they would end up doing things just like what Geir talked about. Watching over somebody who didn't want or need watching over. Over time that could become a problem.

He brought that thought up. "You know? Shepherds need jobs. Malamutes need jobs. Everybody needs something to do, a purpose. I'm wondering, if we have nothing to focus our energies on, will we start crowding, being overprotective, of the women in our lives."

Geir frowned at him. "Did you just call me a dog?"

"I think he called all of us dogs," Erick said with a laugh. "As long as he's the junkyard dog."

But Cade looked at Badger with respect. "I was wondering that myself. We had focus before. We had missions we went on. When we lost all that, we had ourselves to look after, our healing journey to take. We had rehab to do. And then it was hunting down Mouse's life. And here we are, after all that, and we're looking for the next step on our journey."

Badger nodded. "We could set up a security company. Like Levi did."

"We don't have anywhere near the tech experience or equipment or the business location that Levi has though," Cade said.

"No, but it doesn't have to be that kind either," Badger said. "We could do special missions. Contracts from Levi. Even Bullard. I don't know about you guys, but I still have a lot of contacts in the military. We could get involved in a lot of black ops, secret missions."

"Is that what we want to do though?" Talon asked. "We have our women now. Do we want to bring that into their lives?"

And this was where the conversation always ended up. It came right around full circle. They'd already thought about all this, but none of them wanted to leave their women or to expose them to further risk.

"We could do investigative work online. Strictly computer work. We know a lot of people who could use our skills for that."

"Yeah, maybe on a part-time basis. But we've all got that itch to be in the field."

The guys all nodded at that.

"And what about the idea of bringing in other men like us to work with us?" Jager asked.

"We'd have to train them first. That's like creating jobs for other people instead of really for us," Talon joked. "But then we could contract them out to others, like Levi."

"Right, the trouble is, all we do is discuss this. We never get anything mutually finalized."

"There's private law enforcement, bounty hunters," Erick proposed. "You know we'd have no trouble running down the bad guys."

There was silence in the room for a few moments.

"It does sound a little low-level though, doesn't it?" Erick asked, noting the flaw in his idea.

"But it doesn't have to be," Cade said. "It's all about positioning. Brand positioning. Levi handles a lot of secret stuff. We could do the same. We don't have to have the same equipment he does. We could do it on a much smaller scale, more elite. We could hire our services to him and Bullard and to anyone else, like we were talking about, but just keep it small. We don't have to do trips all over the world. Hell, forget working out-of-town altogether. We could work out of our own backyard. I mean, look at Dennis's Santa Fe

Police Department. What happens when a case runs past department capabilities?"

"Well," Jager stated, "from what Allison tells me, the paperwork gets filed and distributed, until something new comes along, but they only really get forty-eight hours to work a case. Plus they have restrictive budgets."

"Sure, but we need money too," Talon said. "We can't do the work for free."

"No, we can't," Badger said. "Yet we keep going back to that. Because that's where our skills are. So, what we need to do is find a way to make something happen so we get paid for what we're doing but can help the community too."

"And that's where we leave it," Erick said. "Everybody needs to think about this. We have the potential for so much. We have unbelievable skills between us." His gaze touched on each and every one of them. "This isn't a case of just *do whatever*. This is a case of finding what each of us wants to do, what our specialties are, and then finding work that we can utilize our skills on." He glanced at Geir. "In the meantime, does Levi need more than one man?"

Badger spoke up. "I hope so because, honestly, I'd rather spend a day standing guard for a lying politician than sitting at home trying to figure out what to do with my life." He said it in a half-joking manner, but he knew the others understood.

Geir nodded at Badger's phone. "Contact Levi and ask him. For all I know, they need all of us."

Badger looked at the phone in his hand. If he contacted Levi, chances were he was taking a step that would direct all the rest of his steps. And those of his buddies' too. It could change everything. Was this what he wanted?

"Better to be brave and make a wrong step," Erick said

beside him, "than to be a coward and never take any step."

He groaned. "Fine. Let me talk to Levi and see what he's looking for." He dialed Levi's number. When his friend answered, he said, "I missed your text earlier. Sorry. What's up?"

"I need a security detail for a government rally."

"They don't have enough manpower in the city?"

"The wife of one of the politicians contacted us. She doesn't trust the city. She thinks something bad is going on."

"What exactly would we be doing?"

"Extra firepower, extra eyes."

"How many are you looking for?"

Levi's voice sounded surprised when he said, "Seven of you, if I can get you all."

"Are you paying?" Badger asked, humor in his voice. "We all owe you as it is, so we'd do the job for free."

"No need," Levi said smoothly. "The wife's paying decently. Besides it's just one day. If you want to take on more work, believe me. I got lots more for you." And he hung up.

The guys looked at each other.

"We didn't get any details yet," Erick noted.

"That's typical of Levi, giving us a moment to think and make a mutual decision." Badger looked at the others. "But this changes things. Just so you all know that. If we take this step, there will be more like this in front of us. Everybody raise a hand to vote."

As he looked around the room, satisfaction swept through him. They'd all raised their hands. Including him. Badger nodded. "Done. I'll call Levi back."

CHAPTER 5

K AT RACED INTO the restaurant.

The waitress waved at her and called out, "The others are already seated."

She nodded and headed to the back room. "May I get a coffee?" she asked.

The waitress, who they all knew as Hindy, nodded and smiled.

Kat walked into the small room to see that, indeed, the other six women were here. She plunked her butt down in the closest empty chair and said, "*Woo!* Didn't think I would make it."

Faith chuckled. "What's this? Like the first time we've all sat down together without the men?"

"Hey, it's not that easy to do," Minx cried out, "with them all at home. But now that they're getting a couple jobs here and there, it should make it easier for us to meet without them catching on."

"I still think they should set up their own company," Allison said.

"It's in progress," Kat said. "At least in the thinking stage. Last I heard, they were considering a high-level umbrella company where they could fine-tune what they wanted to do."

"It's great to be individual contractors for the odd job

for Levi. But to get the insurance and overhead cost covered, they really should have their own umbrella company set up," Faith added.

"How do we feel about the men having a company?" Morning asked.

"It's all good," Kat said.

Honey turned to look at her and said, "I told the others."

"Oh." Kat felt the heat rising up her cheeks. She glanced from one to the other. "It's a crazy idea, isn't it?"

Minx grinned. "I already told you how I feel about it. I think it's great."

Allison chuckled. "It seems too soon to think about marriage—at least in my case—but, if we want to have this all happen at once, it's probably an expedient way to do it."

Faith nodded. "I like that. *Expedient.* Have it all happen at once."

"The thing is, there'll have to be an awful lot of agreement between us all," Kat said.

"Exactly." Honey brought out a pad of paper and a pen. "And some are big issues. We have to pick a day over the long Labor Day weekend, and we can't change it. It can't be changed because there'll be way too much to set in motion. So, it's people like Faith who will have the hardest time juggling that date, keeping it open."

Faith frowned. "Why me?"

"Because you fly on weekends and we were hoping to do it on a weekend, which frees both Kat and me. Morning is painting, so her schedule is a little more flexible. Minx, you start your new job soon, and it'll be a Monday-to-Friday job, right?"

Minx nodded. "Yes, I'll be working at the Women's Crisis Center during the week."

"But could be on-call for weekend emergencies, correct?" Kat asked. "Can you maybe avoid being on-call for that weekend?"

Minx shrugged. "I imagine I can. If it's my wedding, I should be able to," she joked.

"I have time off coming," Faith said. "So I don't think that's an issue for me. I can just book the long weekend off."

"Perfect."

Faith leaned forward. "If we want to do honeymoons, I might be able to help with some flights."

Kat sat back. "Honeymoons. I didn't even give a thought to that."

The others chuckled.

"Chances are we'll do those individually at a later date," Clary said.

"What about Levi and Ice? Have they said anything more?" Honey asked.

Kat shrugged. "I talked to her a couple days ago. She was coming up with a few ideas and so was Levi. When they have something firmed up, they'll get back to us."

"But Labor Day weekend is a go?" Honey asked.

Kat nodded. "So we get together for our surprise whatever midafternoon and have an early evening joint wedding?"

All the women nodded.

"That's probably the easiest," Kat said.

"Depending on what we end up with as an excuse from our end. I'll put an asterisk beside that," Honey said as she wrote down notes.

"If we're all supposed to be ready, we'll need wedding dresses. Is anybody here stuck on a color?" Kat asked.

Morning chuckled. "Growing up, I always wanted

white. But I'm totally open about it."

The women looked at each other.

Faith shrugged. "I have to admit, I was hoping for white."

Kat nodded. "I'm okay with white. Allison, you were married before. Will that be a problem for you?"

Allison shook her head. "I think white would be perfect," she said quietly. "The only thing is, if we're all in white dresses during the day before the ceremony, that's going to be a pretty obvious sign."

"True enough," Kat said. "So, we either have to have all the wedding dresses ready in a spare room, already at my house, so you can all come and get changed there, or the dresses have to be casual enough that we can all get away with it."

"I think whatever we come up with as an excuse, we need to have a reasonable explanation for why there's a photographer," Minx added.

"Clary, do you have anything to add?"

Clary shrugged. "I'm pretty amiable about it all. I never really expected to have the whole white wedding anyway. So I'm pretty jazzed to think I get to now. With Talon."

"And that brings up two issues before I get distracted. Is religion a factor for anybody here?"

"I'm a believer," Faith said, "but I was raised nondenominational and, with my schedule, haven't been to church in eons."

A couple of the women had been raised Catholic but no longer considered themselves as members.

The rest shook their heads.

"So a justice of the peace works for everyone?" Kat asked.

"Sounds good," Minx said, with the others agreeing.

"And the second matter," Kat said, "does anybody have very close family members they want to come for the service?"

The women all settled back as they thought about it, but almost unanimously they shook their heads.

"No, and I think I'd rather take a break and go visit my family later on anyway," Minx said. "My uncle is in Maine. I'd rather pop by and say hi to him on his own terms. Take Laszlo with me."

The others nodded.

Kat asked, "What about having Laszlo's family attend?"

Minx shook her head. "I don't think they're physically in shape for that. Plus that might be another sign to our guys that something big is up."

Clary shrugged. "I don't have any family left. It's just Talon now."

"You have a new family now," Morning said. Impulsively she reached across and gripped Clary's hand. "Don't you forget that," she scolded.

Clary grinned. "Are we really doing this? Are we really putting all seven men on the spot at the same time to get married right then and there?"

Kat stared at all of them. "I really started this just for me. But then Honey thought it was a good idea. And I'm wondering, do we need to do all seven?"

"Yes," Clary said. "These men are bonded in a way I don't think I've ever seen before. And, as such, I think they'll feel left out if one, two, or three of them do this and the others don't. I think they'll also wonder why their girlfriends didn't want this to happen too."

Kat nodded. "That's what I was thinking. Okay, so any

other doubts?"

All the women shared mischievous grins.

"We're all in then?" Kat looked for agreement from each of the women at the table, each raising their hands. "Good. It's unanimous. And it's happening on Labor Day weekend. We all need to decide if we want the same style for our dresses. We're different body types. I think the dresses can be unique to us, but they also need to be relatively similar, at least in formality."

"I think casual summer wedding dresses for a September early evening wedding would be perfect," Faith said. "And, if we're all wearing white, then I suggest we each pick a different color for ribbons, bouquets, whatever, to help distinguish who we are, and we'll have the ties and boutonnieres for the men to match our color."

That brought up a round of *oohs* and *aahs*.

Clary smiled. "May I have peach then please?"

Honey nodded. "I'm okay with you having peach. Anybody else?"

Everybody around the table picked a color. When they finished, the choices were lavender, fuchsia, dark purple, turquoise, peach and then it came to Kat.

Honey looked over at her and said, "I'm going with yellow, and that leaves you. What color would you like to have?"

The corner of Kat's lips twitched. "Anybody got a problem if I go with red?"

At that everyone gave a fat smile.

"Perfect. Style of dress? Leave it open, floor-length, pencil style?" Honey asked.

"Veils? Trains?" Kat added.

Instantly there was a bunch of head shaking. "No trains,

no veils."

"If you want a headpiece, that's fine," Kat said. "And, if you feel really strongly, then speak up because this is your wedding day."

"Did anybody think about what happens if one of the men says no?" Morning asked. "Or if they don't all look absolutely overjoyed and overwhelmed?"

"Is anybody here in doubt of who they want to spend the rest of their life with?" Kat's voice was calm and low. "And I know that's a hard question. We've all come together very fast in a tumultuous way. But I have no doubts myself."

Allison chuckled. "I'm the last one to have joined the group. And our relationship hasn't been but several weeks long. I have more experience, in the sense I was married for a couple years. But I didn't feel this much, this fast even after I married my first husband. Sometimes that makes me feel very guilty."

"I think that's understandable, kinda like survivor's guilt, but you should allow yourself to feel the full happiness of being in love with a great guy. You've been twice blessed," Morning said gently.

"Thank you, Morning. I'll remember that," Allison said with a single nod.

Morning turned back to the others. "We're all agreed this is what we'll do, and we all presume the men will be overjoyed. If not, they'll hide it really well." She laughed with all the others.

"On top of that, we should think about bouquets," Faith said. "Do we want to do seven identical, as to the types and color of the flowers, each with its own respective color of ribbon? Or will they all be a different color and floral combination?"

"I think different, but I want to get back to dresses. Try-ing to get seven of us to agree on a wedding dress would be a little more difficult," Honey said. And then she chuckled. "I have to admit. I've carried this picture around with me for a long time. In fact, Kat and I used to talk about it." She opened up the notepad in front of her to the back page and pulled out a sketch. She handed it around to the others. "That's the wedding dress I have dreamed of all my life."

The women looked at it and nodded.

"It's very simple," Minx said. "I like that. I can't stand ruffles and bows and that God-only-knows-what doodad stuff. I like simple." She tapped the sketch. "Actually, I really like this." She frowned at it slightly. "You know? It would be easy to get everyone an ever-so-slightly different version of this. So we can have our own personality but the same style. Add in a colored bouquet to match the men's boutonnieres, and honestly I think that's great."

She passed it around again, and everybody smiled.

Morning said, "If it'll hold up somebody who's as well-endowed as I am, I'm all for it. Because if I could look slim like that ..."

At that, the other women started in on her.

"Morning, you're perfect just the way you are. You've got curves, girl, and that's something not all of us have," Allison said with a chuckle. "I have more of a boy's figure, and yet that style would also make me look very good." She looked over at Honey. "This is an amazing dress, Honey. Kudos to you for recognizing it so long ago. I got married in a church, and I didn't even have as pretty a wedding dress."

Clary said, "I never expected to get married, so I'm total-ly okay with having a wedding dress at all. But it is pretty, Honey."

"In that case, we need a dressmaker," Honey said. "And, yes, I do have somebody in mind. We also need at least one hairdresser, if not two, for the morning of the wedding."

The women nodded.

"Probably two or three, since there'll be seven of us. And we won't have a very long window to get away with this."

"Maybe three. Maybe one salon that has three really good hairstylists," Honey murmured more to herself.

Kat sat back and watched as all the women joined in. That was one thing about this group. They all had enough independence to be themselves, but they were all easygoing, laid-back gals who understood what really mattered in life, and it had nothing to do with the dresses. It all had to do with the men they were signing up to marry.

"Music?" Kat asked.

The women raised their gazes and frowned.

"No clue," Clary said. "I'm not much of a music person."

"Anybody here a music lover?" Minx asked.

Faith nodded. "I am. I can come up with a repertoire as long as there's nothing you don't hate about it."

"If you'll come up with one," Kat said, "we can all give it a listen and see if there's any changes needed. As long as we don't all go crazy making changes, it should be good."

"Something light, something joyful?" Faith asked.

The others nodded.

Faith sat back. "I'm good with that."

"Food?" Kat asked.

Morning beamed. "I'd say I could do it, but I'm not sure I want to," she confessed.

Kat leaned forward and tapped Honey's pad of paper. "Put Ice down there for me."

Honey looked at her. "Ice doesn't cook."

Kat grinned. "But Alfred does. And Bailey helps run his kitchen."

"Are they good?" Morning asked, chewing on her bottom lip.

Kat looked at her with a smile. "These two people you need to meet."

Morning beamed. "As much as I'd love to do my own wedding, it's a lot of work, and I really want to enjoy the day instead."

"Booze?" And there it went from subject to subject to subject. By the time they got to the guest list, ideas were popping out steadily.

When their lunch arrived, Kat looked at the salad with chunks of chicken in front of her and said, "Did somebody order for me?"

"Of course we did," Honey said with a laugh. "Otherwise you'd never eat."

Kat smiled and dug in. She wasn't sure how she managed to get so lucky. Not only did she have Badger now but she had a ready-made group of warm, caring women friends, something she'd never thought to have and now couldn't imagine life without.

BADGER WALKED IN at the end of the day, dropped his briefcase on the chair in his office, walked upstairs, slipped off his coat and hung it up in the bedroom closet. It had been a long day. He quickly changed into his trunks and headed to the pool.

He walked into the kitchen to see Kat on the phone, a

notepad in front of her.

She glanced up, surprised to see him, smiled and quickly closed the notepad. On the phone call, she said, "I've got to go. Badger is home. Talk to you later." And she hung up really fast.

He frowned, went over and gave her a kiss on the forehead. "Hey, you didn't have to hang up just because I'm home," he protested.

She chuckled. "Not an issue."

But it was. He just didn't know what kind of an issue. Hating secrets, but recognizing it might be a good secret, he headed to the fridge and pulled out a beer. "Plans for dinner?" he asked.

She smiled at him. "Chicken breasts. Cooked somehow. But I was waiting for you to get home. I wasn't expecting you right away. How did it go with the attorney?"

"It was good," he said. "Lots of discussion among the guys. Lots of paperwork handled by the corporate lawyer. We should have a contract to sign in a couple days."

"Now that's awesome," she said. "It's been a long time coming for you guys. What name did you decide on?"

"Titanium Corp. *Men in transition—waterproof, strong, resistant to corrosion … whatever your needs …*"

She stared at him, then smiled. "SEALs are waterproof, you're all definitely strong inside and out, and being the most honorable men I've met you're definitely resistant to corrosion. I love it!"

"And," he said "We're all put back together with Titanium—thanks to you."

"It's perfect," she declared. "And covers the men involved and yet opens up for anything you decide to do. About time."

He laughed. "We just didn't want to jump in until we were ready. Even now we're not exactly clear what we're doing."

"Understood." She got up and pulled out the chicken breasts she had marinating in the fridge. "I've got defrosted and marinated chicken breasts. Just don't know how you might want to cook them."

"We can throw some veggies on skewers and barbecue the whole lot of it," he declared. He grabbed the veggies and started prepping.

She smiled and stepped up to work beside him. They worked quietly together for several minutes. "Isn't Talon's birthday in September, close to yours?" she asked suddenly.

"He's the seventh of September." He looked at her in surprise. "Why?"

"Just wondering," she said.

He shrugged. "I think a couple more of us are in September."

"Really?"

Something odd was in her tone. He nodded. "Why?"

"Just might be nice to have a big party."

He thought about it and agreed. "I'm always up for a party. Especially if it's with the guys."

She laughed. "Isn't that the truth."

"Is that okay?"

"Absolutely, it's okay," she said. "Maybe, if there are multiple birthdays, we should invite some outside people too?"

"Go for it," he said. "Invite who you want."

She beamed at him. "You know? You're very generous."

He wrapped an arm around her shoulder, kissed her gently on the temple and said, "If you're happy, I'm happy."

She reached up and kissed him lightly on the lips. "Hope you don't regret saying that."

He laughed out loud. "Okay, now you're scaring me. What are you up to?"

"Oh, I was thinking about doing a surprise party, but I figured you wouldn't like the surprise. So, I thought if I brought it up, maybe you'd be okay with me planning a big party. But it'll still be a surprise birthday party for the other birthday boys, okay?"

"Sure, and you're right. I can't say that surprises are anything I'm fond of, so thank you for letting me know."

"Are you okay if I handle it?"

"Absolutely. The less I have to do with it, the better."

She chuckled. She walked over to her notepad, picked it up and put it into the drawer to the side of the fridge. "I'll finish up the veggies. You want to light the barbecue?"

He nodded and headed for the grill. From the corner of his eye, he watched as she pulled out the pad of paper and wrote down a couple notes. He was much happier and more at ease thinking that a surprise party had been in the back of her mind. He wasn't the kind to really enjoy a surprise like that. He struggled with change. He struggled with a lot of things. And the fact that she hadn't tried to pull something like that on him made him feel all that much better. And, besides, a surprise party wasn't a bad thing. Particularly as several of the guys did have birthdays in September, and he thought one or two might be in August. They could have one hell of a birthday party bash. He smiled, liking the idea all the more.

Soon she stepped out to the barbecue area with two platters, one of chicken and the other of skewered veggies. He put them on the hot grill and asked, "Will you enjoy planning something like this, or is it too much for you to do alone?"

"I would love to plan it." She looked around the back-yard. "I was trying to figure out how much space you had here, whether a party would work outside or not."

He grinned, feeling the last of his worries dropping away. That's why the woman was here. "I did see somebody out back here with a measuring tape," he admitted.

Sheepishly she said, "Yeah, she came because I couldn't give her dimensions. She thought she'd run by and take a quick look. She said she knocked but didn't get an answer, so she came around back for a quick set of measurements."

"Do you need to hire help?"

She laughed. "No, she's a friend of mine. She really likes to do this kind of stuff. But I will admit, she probably overstepped her boundaries by coming and measuring. I could have done that whenever I got a chance."

"You do what makes this fun for you. And thank you for telling me. I promise I won't tell the rest of them."

"Good. There could be maybe five of you all having birthdays within a couple months. That sounds like a pretty decent excuse for a party to me. I'd like to do it on Labor Day weekend."

He thought about it. "That might be doable. We have enough advance notice to not take on any jobs that might come in that weekend."

"Can you handle making excuses to the guys? Even though you know, I still want to make it a surprise for the others."

He thought about it and nodded. "I need to have a good reason though. That doesn't spoil your surprise."

She stared at him hopefully. "But you could, couldn't

you?"

He sighed. "I'll figure it out," he promised.

When she beamed at him, he realized just how bad he had it. Anything that made her happy, made him happy. God, he sounded like a lovesick puppy. But what he really was, was a man in love. He reached out an arm and held her close. "If you want to bring in some outside guests, you could offer a couple of our bedrooms here," he said. "Just don't make it too many."

She laughed, wrapping her arms around him. "Have I told you that I love you?"

"You have," he said, his voice thickening. "But not today." She looked up, her eyes huge pools that he could drown in. They were so open, so welcoming and so full of love, he wondered how he'd ever gotten so lucky. He lowered his head and kissed her gently. "You know? If we hadn't already loaded up the barbecue ..."

She reached up and tugged his ear. "After dinner. You know there's absolutely no shortage of time to see me."

"So, pool after that?"

"Pool after that," she confirmed. She chuckled and said, "I think I smell something burning."

Swearing, he turned back to the grill.

CHAPTER 6

FOR THE THIRD Tuesday in a row, Kat raced into the restaurant late. As she arrived, she plunked down beside Honey. "How do you get here so fast?" Kat wailed. "I do my damnedest to make it on time, and I never seem to get there."

Honey looked at her friend and grinned. "How long before you realize my office is around the corner?"

Kat looked at her and blinked, then blinked again. She shook her head. "Wow. Why didn't I think of that?"

"Because you're a little bit crazy-busy in your mind."

She'd already shared Badger's suggestion about keeping the massive surprise birthday party a secret from all the guys but not from him. The others had loved the idea. Last week they'd worked on wedding-related details: flower arrangements, music themes, decorating themes. It all had to be done, knowing it was a wedding for seven couples in the guise of a surprise birthday party for five guys.

So, as soon as one person got a little too far on the wedding theme line, somebody else had to pull them back. But so far, the ideas were gelling nicely.

Morning walked in just then. "I talked to Ice. While we know about the proposal setup, Levi hasn't told Badger yet. But Ice promised that Levi is calling Badger today to set that in motion. Also she suggested that Alfred and Bailey come with them to New Mexico to help with the food prep. Even stating that much could be done in advance and could come with them, already prepared."

"Yes, but where can they set up?" Kat asked.

"You've got the biggest kitchen, Kat," Honey said quietly.

"Exactly."

"And I've got the smallest," Morning said. "But we could split it up among our homes."

Kat nodded. "Badger did say I could bring a few people in."

"Good enough. But we still don't have a reason to get the men in suits for our supposed big birthday bash."

"No, we don't," Minx said. "But I think just suits and no tuxes."

"We couldn't get them fitted for a tux if we don't have our own reason to get them so formally set up," Clary said.

The women all sat back and thought about it.

"All the guys really like Levi, don't they?" Allison asked.

Kat nodded. "Not to mention they were a huge help over this last nightmare with Mouse. So, if Levi asked them to wear suits, or even tuxes, they would definitely do it."

"But is going formal Levi's style?" Minx asked worriedly.

"Ice did mention something like that. Levi said he would kidnap her for a honeymoon. But, because it would be completely out of the norm, he would do something like the formal engagement party because she wouldn't be expecting it."

"Wow, three secret parties all rolled into one production," Honey said, her eyes wide and on Kat.

Understanding slowly dawned on all their faces.

"That's pretty cool actually," Minx said. "So, after's Levi

call to Badger today, all the men dress up for Levi, knowing that, at the surprise engagement/birthday/wedding party—depending on which group you are in—he's going to ask Ice to marry him. And of course there's absolutely no way she'd say no, so the guys all dress up and make this a big to-do. Lucky for Badger, Kat wants to do a big surprise birthday bash for the five birthday guys, which serves as Ice's surprise engagement party too, because the guys won't tell us about Levi's proposal for fear we couldn't keep *that* secret. But the men will all know what this is about, so they'll all be grinning and smirking."

Clary leaned forward. "And that's a perfect excuse for having the photographer there."

"In the meantime, Ice has to pretend to be completely ignorant about it," Morning said. "Well, and us too."

"As to the supposed proposal. But Ice won't be because she'd be part of this whole scheme to get our men there to get married," Kat said triumphantly. "What do you guys think?"

Unanimously the women nodded.

"I think it'll work. I like it," Faith said. "You know something? The men won't know what hit them."

They all laughed.

"So we still have other things to take care of, right?" Kat asked.

"Yes, food is a big one," Honey said, checking her notepad.

They looked over at Morning.

"Did you get a chance to come up with a menu?" Kat looked hopefully at Morning.

She shrugged. "I've got a list of things to suggest," she said hesitantly. "And I'm trying to find items we can have beforehand, and then fancier items we can have afterward."

"Oh, that's a good idea," Clary said. "If we have really fancy stuff beforehand, the men will get suspicious."

"Exactly. And the real interesting thing here," Kat said, "is how the men need to get *us* dressed up for this supposed big surprise party," she said quietly, "without telling us anything about Ice's pending proposal in all of this. I can't wait to see what Badger comes up with."

Merriment crossed their faces.

"So, we need prewedding clothes," Allison said. "And we need wedding dresses. And what about after the wedding?"

"Well, if our wedding dresses aren't these huge billowing things with trains, then we can wear them throughout the evening too," Faith suggested. "But let's focus on food first."

Morning quickly read off a few suggestions. "For the informal buffet beforehand, we keep it to finger foods, maybe ribs, maybe sliders, little desserts, individual cupcakes. But not too much. And then, after the wedding, I suggest we bring out things like canapés, maybe mini-cheesecakes. Fancier finger food again instead of a big sit-down dinner. My stomach will be completely knotted up until the final reveal, so I won't eat too much beforehand."

"*The final reveal.*" Kat rolled that idea around on her tongue. "I love it. I think that's what we should call this episode of our lives. The great reveal."

"Maybe the great trick," Faith said with one raised eyebrow. "I have to admit. I'm still a little worried."

"You don't need to be," Morning said gently. "Cade is completely head over heels in love with you."

"I know," she said. "But it does feel like we're putting them on the spot, maybe tricking them."

"If he did this to you, how would you feel?" Allison

asked. "In my case, I'd be absolutely thrilled. But I think the guys are the ones who don't feel 100 percent whole, and a part of them thinks we could do better. So we need to step up and set the matter straight."

Faith nodded. "Absolutely," she said. "And I'm not backing out. Don't get me wrong. I really want this, but I want all the guys to be overjoyed. I want them overwhelmed, ecstatic, and I want them to fall in love with us all over again."

Silence fell as the women thought about all that.

Kat smiled. "And I think that's exactly what'll happen. Of course, we might need more booze."

BADGER STARED INTO the phone receiver. "So, hang on a second. I know there was talk about you coming soon, in another month or so."

"Now we're delaying it to Labor Day weekend. Kat said you're having a big party then."

"And of course you're totally welcome," Badger said, grinning. "It'll be great to see you."

"We don't want to gate-crash," Levi said modestly.

"Hell, I think Kat was looking for an end-of-summer excuse for a big party. The fact that you're coming makes that excuse all the more viable."

"Maybe." There was hesitation in Levi's voice.

"What's going on?"

Levi groaned. "I'm planning on doing something that's completely out of character, and I'm really afraid it'll blow up in my face," he said hurriedly.

Badger relaxed in his chair, propping his good leg on the

top of his desk. "This sounds interesting. The big bad Levi? What's got you scared?"

Levi took a deep breath and said, "I'm thinking about asking Ice to marry me."

Badger just stared across the room, a huge grin breaking across his face. "Hot damn! Now that would be a reason for a party."

"Actually I was wondering if we could make use of your party, and maybe we could dress up a little bit …" Levi said.

Badger could hear the hesitation in his voice.

"… and I could spring the question at the party."

Badger got up and paced the room. "I think that's an absolutely fantastic plan," he cried out. "Ice will be thrilled."

"But will she?" Levi asked. "Especially if I do it publicly?"

"Well, you can definitely count on her saying yes that way."

Levi laughed. "I have to admit that's kind of why I was thinking of doing it this way. It's a little bit unnerving to think she might say no. But, if she's surrounded by friends and family, who know how close we are, then I suspect she'll say yes."

"You know what? I think she'd also like the grand gesture."

"Really? Because I was thinking that she'd probably expect something quiet, with dimmer lights and maybe in the middle of the night."

"Maybe, but she's very much somebody who likes gestures. So this would be completely over-the-top."

"I know," Levi said with a note of dread in his voice. "And I'm definitely on the nervous side."

"Got it. So, what would you like us to do?"

"I was hoping to go a bit formal. No tuxes or anything. Just suits for us guys. Plain black. We all have one, right? And Ice has almost no occasion to dress up, yet I know she loves to. She has this absolutely darling little sleeveless dress in gold. She was hoping for an excuse to wear it. And I could provide all the booze," Levi said hurriedly.

Badger chuckled. "That could be a lot of booze."

Levi laughed. "Maybe, but this is an engagement party, and nobody knows about it yet."

"Can I tell the guys?"

Levi hesitated. "You can tell the guys but not the girls. I can't take the chance of it getting back to Ice. She's incredibly astute. And, if the women have any idea, Ice will know instantly."

Badger thought about that and nodded. "I think you're quite right there. Ice reads people like there's no tomorrow."

"Exactly," Levi said, relief in his voice. "But the thing is, we're kind of gate-crashing your place. It's almost like I should throw a big party here."

Badger shook his head. "Nah. We've already got our party in place. Besides, you can have the wedding at your place. That whole family of yours there in Houston will be pissed off if you don't."

"God, can you imagine?" Levi groaned. "It's one thing to be in the doghouse with Ice, but to be in the doghouse with all those other women? That would be scary."

"Absolutely. So do you want to come that weekend then, and we'll do this, what, Saturday night?"

"Yeah, and, if you're okay with that, we'll stay Sunday, maybe drive home on Monday."

"You got it, absolutely. I'll tell Kat you're coming, and we'll save you a room."

"Yeah. Alfred was talking about coming too. But I don't know."

"Hey, if he wants to come and help out with the food, he's more than welcome. Actually, I shouldn't even put that on him. Alfred does so much cooking for so many as it is. He could just need the time off."

Levi said, "I'll run it past him, see what he says. Bailey is here if he's gone for a few days."

"You're right. Maybe Bailey needs to come too," Badger said, laughingly. "Depending on how big this party will be, I might need a catering service."

Levi chuckled. "I hear ya." As he went to end the call, he stopped and said, "Badger?"

"Yeah? What's up?"

"Thanks." And Levi hung up.

Badger stared down at the phone, grinning like a madman.

Just then Kat walked in. She took one look at the big grin. "Well, you're in a happy mood."

He shrugged and tried to school his features to not reveal his mischievous six-year-old side.

"What's up?"

He shrugged. "No idea. Why? Something up with you?"

She stared at him suspiciously for a long moment, her toes tapping on the floor. "I'm heading into the pool for a swim."

He nodded. "I'll join you in a few minutes." As soon as he heard her footsteps retreating, he got up, walked to the doorway and checked to see that she went to the pool as she had said. Then he went back to his phone and dialed. "Erick, holy crap, have we got some fun coming." And he quickly explained. "So all the guys need to know, but none of the women. Got that?"

Erick laughed aloud. "You know how hard it'll be to keep that secret for weeks from our women who can read us like any profiler?"

Badger stared out at the water where Kat swam, watching her strong strokes as she powered through the water. "Oh, yeah. It'll be so damn hard. But just think of the payout."

"Levi and Ice? Damn, it's about time," Erick said. "I'm calling Laszlo right now."

"You do that. I'll call Cade." Badger hung up and called Cade, relaying the news. "Now remember. The women aren't to know a thing."

Cade chuckled. "You know? I think I even have a black suit somewhere around here. Time to pull out that sucker and see if it still fits."

"I don't know if I do or not. We've all changed shapes. I might have to hit a tailor to see about it."

"Perfect. We'll be Levi's support team. And I gotta tell you. I'm looking forward to seeing Levi pop the question. Nice to know he can get nervous too. He's the absolute top of the top, best of the best, the most confident man in the world," Cade said. "And I mean that in the very best way."

When Badger hung up, he thought about it, realizing it would be a whole new role for Levi because that man knew his shit. But, when it came to women, Badger didn't think there was a man alive who truly understood them.

CHAPTER 7

I T WAS HARD for Kat to get through each and every day. The pressure was building inside; the number of decisions to be made were even greater than she had expected. It was bad enough to plan one wedding but seven weddings? And seven weddings without the grooms' knowledge? Kat didn't know why she had even considered planning such a potential nightmare. And yet, at the same time, she desperately wanted it to work.

The women were gathered on yet another week at their regular place, their discussions hot and heavy, as they'd gone over food, took into consideration special diets and had a menu, more or less, hammered out.

"Did anybody contact Alfred about this?"

Automatically everybody turned to look at Kat.

She shook her head. "No. I haven't," she confessed. "But I know Ice is on it."

"We'll need to contact a catering company for dishes, silverware, table setups," Morning said.

Kat's stomach twisted and turned, and she felt sick. "We don't have enough time to get all this done," she cried out.

Honey reached a hand over to touch Kat's. "Yes, we do. It doesn't matter if things aren't perfect. We have enough time to get us all married. That's the most important thing." She glanced around. "Did anybody stop at the florist?"

Faith nodded. "I had the last couple days off, and I'm flying out tomorrow. But I stopped by and picked up these." She sent pictures of flowers around the table. "This is a fairly standard bouquet, but they did a sample in each color for us. And what we could do is have them trailing down a bit or have them each slightly different."

Clary picked up the one with the peach-colored flowers and sighed happily. "This is so pretty."

The others nodded.

"They're beautiful," Minx said.

"The thing is, we made some decisions about the kind of flowers, but they couldn't get all of our flowers in the right shades," Faith added.

"I don't know that it matters. They don't have to be the same kinds of flowers." Clary stared at the deep turquoise-colored flowers in the picture in her hand. "Because this is absolutely stunning. But obviously these are very different flowers than what Minx has."

Minx nodded. "But, when you see it like this, you want it."

Faith chuckled. "I'm sure that's why they do it this way. Matching boutonnieres for the men." Then she named a price.

The women looked at her.

"Is that for each bride?" Clary asked hesitantly.

Faith nodded. "I know. It's high, right?"

The women were silent for a long moment.

Clary shrugged. "I don't care. I love this. I'm totally okay to pay that."

"But it's adding up, isn't it? We can't make this happen for less than three grand each, and it might be closer to five apiece total," Honey said.

Minx winced. "I'm probably the worst off financially of all of us," she said. "Five thousand is a lot for me."

Kat said, "It's a lot for any of us, and we're trying to keep it as low as possible. The dresses are the biggest expense. Some women spend an unbelievable amount of money on their wedding dress."

"I did swing by the dressmaker's last week," Honey said. "I showed her the sketches we went over. I said it would be seven women, seven fittings, with some small finite details to make each our own." She brought up the sketches that the woman had done for her. "Suggestions for details that would make it our own are things like going strapless, or this one has a jewel collar with a piece coming down across the bosom." She held them up and explained. "All of these are fairly minor things that can be added but will make each dress unique. What do you think?"

After that, the discussion centered around types of fabric, designs, time for fittings, etc.

Kat admitted she felt like she was drowning.

Allison looked over at her. "And work is really busy for you too, isn't it?"

"It always is," Kat said, shifting in her chair so she could lean back a little more comfortably. "But then what about you?"

"I have a job interview tomorrow," Allison admitted. "I'll be in a different department than my brother. But, with any luck, I'll be employed again very quickly."

"Is that what you want to do?" Kat asked.

"Yes, for the moment," Allison said. "It's what I was trained to do. Down the road, maybe that'll change. But this lets me land gently and have a regular paycheck." She nodded toward the sketches. "None of this will be cheap, and I didn't have much of a savings account to begin with."

Kat nodded. "To a certain extent, most of us are in a similar boat."

The sketches reached Allison's area of the table, and Kat could see them while Allison held them out enough for the two of them.

Kat smiled. "I'm tall enough to wear all of this, but I'm struggling with the shoes decision."

The women frowned at her.

"I do have a prosthetic," she said with a laugh. "I have a dress leg. If I could find a particular matching shoe, that would be perfect."

Honey nodded. "I'm sure we could find something. There has to be some individuality among us."

"And we're doing a lot of that, just by being who we are. Like a flick of a stroke of color can change everything," Morning said with a smile.

"Says the painter," Minx teased. "Can you take time off for this wedding when you've got that show coming up?"

Morning flushed. "Sometimes I can't paint at all. I get caught up in daydreams about this, and then I get scared, and I start to paint something totally different," she admitted.

"I wonder if that isn't something we're all going through," Faith said. "Sometimes, when I'm flying across the continent, I'm thinking things, like, he so won't be happy with me about this."

"I think we're all feeling that," Kat said. "But we've gone so far down this road now, it would be hard to change it."

"Particularly with the fake engagement party happening," Honey joked. "We owe Levi big time for that."

Kat grinned. "Badger took his black suit out of the closet

the other day and said he would take it to the dry cleaners the next time he was in town. I looked at him like I was surprised, and he shrugged and just said, *You never know when you might need one.*"

The others all laughed.

"I don't even think Jager has a suit, black or any other color," Allison said, frowning. "How the hell am I going to get him into one?"

"I was thinking about something else," Clary said hesitantly. "And, for the life of me, I can't find a solution."

Everyone turned to look at her.

When she didn't say anything, Kat raised an eyebrow. "Clary, what's up?"

She leaned her arms on the table and clasped her hands in front of her. "Did anybody think about rings?" She was hesitant to bring it up.

Silence descended.

Kat nodded. "I have been. But haven't a clue how to make it work."

"I'm not sure there's anything we can do about them," Honey said slowly. "And that's really a shame." She looked around at the others. "I would like to have a wedding ring."

Minx thrummed her fingers on the table. "Well, there's no reason not to do wedding rings. What we can't do for ourselves is engagement rings."

"We could," Morning said. "There's a real trend toward shared engagement rings. Although I prefer the traditional way, such as what Levi is trying to do as an excuse to have everybody come for the party."

"Right, the big engagement party so he can ask Ice."

"We can certainly do rings for the men and, at the same time, for ourselves."

"I'm not sure I would want an engagement ring any-way," Kat said quietly. "Not to be difficult or anything, but, with my work, I'd have to take it off all the time."

Honey nodded. "Same for me. A wedding ring at least is slim fitting, but anything that's big or bulky isn't something I want around a patient's mouth."

"That brings up a multitude of opinions on what we're doing and the way we're doing it," Faith said.

"Nothing is stopping the men from buying us diamond rings after the fact," Clary said with a laugh. "We're already being nontraditional. Nobody has the right to say what's right or wrong when it comes to something like this. But what we do need is rings for the ceremony."

Everybody sat in silence, drinking coffee and finishing their lunch.

"We have a good long list of things to deal with going forward as it is," Honey said. "We all need to get to the dressmaker for measurements to be taken. Everybody has to go to the florist to clear their bills for the final arrangements for the boutonnieres and bouquets." She paused for a moment. "And we have to confirm the food."

"The problem with the food is," Morning said quietly, "I don't think we'll get a catering company to handle it at this late hour."

"In that case, maybe we just don't need as much. You know the guys. They're totally happy to have steaks on the grill," Kat said with a laugh.

"True enough. Why are we trying to make it so fancy?" Minx said. "Really, we don't have to."

Morning nodded thoughtfully. "You know? I could do a lot ahead of time, particularly if I could get Alfred and Bailey to help. Let me think about that. I was thinking of fancy fare, but I'm not sure that's what we want."

The women instinctively shook their heads.

"I'll let you know. Soon."

"Great. So it'll be black suits, wedding dresses, flowers, etc., and we haven't decided on booze yet either," Honey said. "So it'd be good to have nice food. But I don't think we have to go over-the-top expense-wise. None of us are flush and need that extra money going out the window. We also haven't come up with a full guest list. And, if we're talking more than fifty or sixty additional people, you know we're talking a lot of food."

"Well, there'll be dozens of us here locally for sure," Allison said. "And I'd love to have my brother and his wife and kids there, if that's all right."

"Absolutely. You're one of the few of us who has family close by."

Allison smiled. "And I don't get to see Dennis very much. I've seen him twice since I've arrived. But I think he'd be devastated to find out I got married and didn't invite him. On the other hand, he might be devastated to find out how I'm getting married." She laughed.

Just then Hindy stepped up and said, "Look, ladies. You know I've heard bits and pieces of your discussions over the last few weeks. You do know we cater too, right?"

They were silent as everybody digested that. They looked over at Morning, and she looked at Hindy with a narrowed gaze. "I suppose you have a menu and price list I could take home and consider?"

Hindy nodded. "I'll get you something. Hang on a minute." And she left.

"If nothing else," Morning said, leaning closer, "we could at least take a look at what they offer. But, if we don't plan too much, I think Alfred and Bailey can do most of it."

"Plus the food detail won't land just on you," Clary said. "I'm nowhere near the magic you are in the kitchen, but we can all pitch in and help."

"The trouble is, it'll be hard to do that, whether a secret or not," Morning said. "None of us really has the kitchen space."

"So maybe catering is the answer," Clary said. "I'm happy to pitch in a little more money to make something like that happen."

"Me too," Morning added.

Instantly there were cries of outrage.

Clary chuckled. "I'm not exactly broke. Remember?"

"And I just sold my B and B, remember?" Morning said.

"Doesn't matter," Kat said. "This wedding ceremony is for each of us. I suggest we get clear with Alfred first. Then, if we need more help, we'll consider the options."

"Sounds good. And won't we have an interesting anniversary every year." Honey laughed out loud. "Talk about an annual party."

The women all grinned.

Just then Hindy returned with information that she handed to Morning.

"How much advance notice do you need for orders?" Morning asked, studying the sheets. "Just so we have an idea of our options."

"Obviously the earlier, the better. You're talking Labor Day weekend, if I'm correct?"

The women nodded.

"And that, of course, is a busy weekend. But that doesn't mean we can't do something for you."

"I'll let you know." Morning sat back with the sheets in

front of her. "What if they did the more involved stuff, and we could do the easier stuff? Like, we could bring the salads, fresh buns and fresh breads ordered from that little Swiss bakery."

"Desserts?"

Morning chuckled. "Desserts are mandatory."

"Let me talk to Ice to see what Alfred and Bailey might do to help out. According to Badger, Bailey loves baking."

"Exactly," Morning said, continuing to study the sheets. "I need to think about this." She glanced around the room. "None of us having a large-enough kitchen is the big problem. But leave it with me, and I'll talk to Alfred and Ice."

"Mine's probably the biggest," Kat admitted. "And I'm one of the least able to make magic in there."

Morning smiled. "It's not hard to make magic in the kitchen. And, once you get started, it's amazingly easy to create more and more magic."

Kat knew what Morning meant, but she was wrong when it came to Kat. Morning was seriously talented. "We haven't talked about booze," Kat announced. "First off, Levi offered to bring the booze, but I'm not sure what kinds. Anyone have a preference?"

"Well, we've talked about it, but we haven't decided anything." Honey looked up from her notepad. "I would like champagne."

The women all nodded.

"Do we want to keep it to several glasses of champagne, then switch to wine or to the hard stuff? Or do we drink champagne all night or ..." Honey's voice ran down.

"If cost is an issue, we can toast with champagne, but we'll need to shift to something else afterward," Kat said.

DALE MAYER

"Then again I don't buy a whole lot of booze, but there's a lot of beer in my house." She laughed. "And honestly I think Badger might prefer a beer."

"He'll probably want a whiskey afterward," Minx said beside her. "As I recall, the men all drink beer and then the hard stuff. But they're not so much into mixed drinks."

That brought up a lively discussion of what the women wanted to drink.

Honey kept writing down suggestions and ideas. "We're looking at least one if not two grand on the booze. Is that fair to Levi?"

"It all depends on how many bodies are coming," Kat said. "So we have to get that guest list finalized, then tell Levi and let him decide on quantities."

"I'm sitting at forty-seven total at the moment, based on everybody's guest list," Faith said. "Including us." She brought out her notepad. "And that's not tons. That's a fairly small wedding."

"Small is better," Clary said. "I mean, think about it. So many of us don't even have family."

The women nodded.

"What about the justice of the peace?"

Just then Kat's phone rang. She glanced down and said, "I'm running late." She stood, pulled cash out of her wallet, dropped it on the table and smiled at the ladies. "We're running out of weeks. You all know that, right?"

Solemnly, they all nodded.

"We may need two lunches a week until we've got this all locked down," Honey said.

"I'll get to the dressmaker and to the florist this week," Kat said. "If I need to do anything else, send me an email, will you?" And she dashed out of the restaurant.

Kat stood outside for a long moment. Her heart was so full, and yet she was so terrified. They were really doing this. But was it the right thing to do?

BADGER SAT AT Talon's kitchen table, with the rest of the guys milling about. "Okay, so we have three jobs lined up. Do we need more men, or are we good?"

"I think, because the three jobs are staggered," Erick said logically, "we should be fine."

"Did the extra weapon licenses come through yet?" Laszlo said.

"They did," Talon said. "We have to pick them up tomorrow."

"Okay, so we've got one two-man job. We've got a one-man job, and we've got a three-man job. So that doesn't seem like we have much of a problem with manpower."

"Exactly what I was thinking," Badger said.

Just then Jager stepped in and waggled his phone in his hand. "Except that we have a fourth job. Levi needs a hand. He needs two hands actually."

"Two hands or two sets of hands?" Erick asked, clarifying.

Jager chuckled. "Two sets. Brandon is coming to New Mexico on a job, but they don't have any spare men to back him up. Kasha is over in England. They're hoping we've got a couple people who can join Brandon."

"What's he doing?"

"A bounty hunter picked up a runaway. Lost him. The bounty hunter ended up in the hospital. He called Levi for help."

"Wow, bounty hunters calling Levi now?"

"The bounty hunter didn't want to admit it," Jager said, "but he got taken in pretty good. Levi is sending in Brandon, but Levi needs to ensure Brandon has backup. This guy is a prepper. Lots of weapons." Jager groaned. "And, as a complete aside, but I need to bring it up before I forget, I did a survey of the veteran list we were looking at and their list of trades. We need to get organized and figure out what we want to do there."

"Later," Badger said. "We've got a lot going on now."

After that, the discussion settled into who wanted to go where and do what job.

By the time they had that sorted out, Badger sat back, popped the top off another beer and said, "Do you guys all have suits?"

They each nodded.

"I do. Probably need to take it to the dry cleaners though," Jager said. "It's not fancy though."

"Sure it is. If it's black, it's fancy enough," Laszlo said. "We've all got black suits. We don't need more than that, do we?" He turned to look at Badger.

"I don't think so," Badger said. "A black suit is good for everything." His tone turned morose. Because, of course, most of them had picked up a black suit for funerals. The only other time they really needed them was for weddings. But there hadn't been any of those in their lives in a long time.

Jager said, "I can't believe Levi is going to pop the question."

"I know." Badger looked around at the other guys. "Any of you thought about it?"

Erick shrugged. "Of course I've thought about it. Just

haven't done anything about it."

Cade laughed. "Me too. I think that's probably the same for all of us. You realize that, once Levi does this, the girls will likely look at us."

"Or maybe not," Geir said. "Let's not forget Levi and Ice have been together for literally years."

"In a way he's well past time," Badger said.

"We all have pretty new relationships. Comparatively."

Silence fell.

Badger said quietly. "My relationship with Kat has gone farther and faster than anything I've ever had before."

"Ours was pretty intense as far as the courtship went," Jager said. "Allison and I are still getting used to living in the same space."

"But it's a fun process, isn't it?" Laszlo asked, shooting him a big grin.

Jager laughed. "It so is. And, down the road, marriage is something we'll all have to consider."

"Thankfully that's down the road," Erick said. "I want time to just think about the joy of what I have without jeopardizing it by asking a question that maybe my partner isn't ready for."

"That's the thing, right? Our women are the ultimate career professionals. Clary too, even though she's not looking for a job, she's rethinking her work as a paralegal. Maybe they don't like weddings. Maybe marriage isn't in their future," Badger said. "I can honestly say I've never even broached the subject."

"Are you kidding? That's like opening a huge yawning pit. No matter what you say, you'll say it wrong," Geir said. "Some avenues of discussion you just don't go down until you're ready to take the plunge."

The men chuckled, but they all nodded in agreement.

"Does Levi need us to do anything else except be fully dressed?"

"No, the problem is, whether we can get the women to dress up," Laszlo said, "without having to explain."

"Yeah, I know. Not all of them necessarily like dressing up either."

"True enough. I'm not sure Allison is into high heels," Jager said. "I'm not even sure she moved any evening clothes with her."

"Same with Morning."

"I think, in each case," Badger said, "they probably have something that will look nice. But, if we're expecting this to be superformal, not one of them will appreciate us not giving them a heads-up. Apparently that's really important to women."

"So, do we tell them it'll be a formal affair and to find some glad rags to put on?" Talon asked.

"I think we need to nudge them somewhat. We can't tell them any details though."

"Is Levi telling Ice?"

"Only that it's formal. And, if she doesn't bring the gold dress, he's planning on packing it for her."

"Ice in gold." Talon shook his head. "That'll be something to see."

"I'm really happy for them," Badger said suddenly. "They're good people."

"They sure are," Lazlo said, shaking his head. "It'll be a hell of a wedding at their compound."

"I know. And we might get invitations," Badger said with a laugh. "And, if that's the case, I'm definitely going."

The others nodded.

"Even if it's just to see how their operation runs," Geir added. "They've got the setup. They've got the location. They've got the proper buildings. It's a bloody fortress down there."

"We have to start small," Erick said, focusing on the logistics. "Taking on little jobs, doing a few things here and there. If it gets bigger than that, we'll need to look for a central location ourselves."

"Could be just an office though, a storefront for meetings with clients or whatever," Badger said. "We could all have home offices and work from there."

"Well, you know one thing is for sure," Talon said. "None of us needs a helicopter, like Ice insists on."

"But she runs it pretty heavily too," Badger said. "According to Levi, when times were tough, her helicopter pilot skills kept them bringing in the money."

"Makes sense," Talon agreed. "They're very diverse."

"And we need to maintain diversity too," Cade noted. "If we see ourselves going too far in one direction, we need to pull back and keep sprawling out in other directions. We can bring on other people if we want to, but the seven of us need some kind of steady employment."

"And the paycheck is not the big deal. We're all getting solid pensions, so it's not like we're starving. But we all need that sense of contributing in some way." Erick smiled at the rest of them. "It's hard to let go of being a hero."

"That's the thing," Talon said. "I think, to the women, we'll always be heroes."

Cade added, "And that's a damn nice feeling."

"What about booze for the party?" Talon asked, looking at Badger. "Did Levi say anything about that?"

"He's picking up booze for the party. I think he had

some decent-size budget in mind."

"So, champagne?"

"He asked me about that. I thought we should probably have a couple cases, and then we can switch out to hard drinks or wine."

"Okay, sounds good. What about food?"

Badger was stumped. "I don't know. The thing is, Kat was looking at doing this party all on her own, and now we've kind of boosted it, so I need to talk to her about that." He checked his watch and stood. "I guess I can do that in about ten minutes when I get home," he joked. "Are you guys keeping track of the time?"

With a wave goodbye, Badger walked out the front door of Talon's house and headed home. His mind was full because Kat had been so excited about this, and he didn't want to take the thrill away from her. But, because of Levi's thing, it had gotten a whole lot bigger fast.

As he walked in, she was coming out of the kitchen, a big cookie in her fingers. He glanced at the cookie and smiled. "You're just lucky I saved you one," he joked.

She nodded, reached up and kissed him gently. "I was going to ask, now that we've got Levi coming, maybe we could get Alfred and possibly Bailey on board to bring in some food? But maybe that's not fair if Levi is picking up the booze. Plus Alfred and Bailey cook for everyone at the compound every day, right?"

Badger had to think about that. "I know, but Morning is too busy, painting for her upcoming show, and there'll be a bigger crowd now, so we might need to get some catering brought in."

"I'll talk to Ice first, then get on the catering issue if needed."

He grinned with relief. "That's perfect. You know we could just go with burgers." He tossed her a grin as he headed out to the pool.

"We're not having burgers," she called out. "No way. We have those damn-near every Sunday as it is."

"No, we don't. We had ribs last Sunday," he said.

She chuckled, following him to the pool. "What are we having this Sunday?" she teased.

He spun around to look at her. "Talon is bringing some special chicken dish."

Her smile kicked up a few degrees. "You know? I really like that. It's not just all on us each Sunday."

He shook his head. "That's what friends do. Everybody brings something, and then it's not such a headache for anyone, and we rotate the meat around so nobody's bored with hamburgers, and it works."

She nodded and sat in her lounger. "It's been a long day."

"I called you at lunchtime," he said, casting her a glance.

"Yeah, I went out with the girls today."

"The girls?" He watched a flush cross her face.

"We've gotten in the habit of having lunch together."

He studied her for a long moment. "All of you?"

She nodded. "At least as many as can make it on the day." She hesitated. "Is that okay?"

He stared at her for a long moment and thought about what he'd hoped for with the women's relationships. "I think it's way better than okay," he admitted. "I think it's frickin' perfect."

She beamed, hopped up and walked toward him. "After the Mouse crisis was over, I was afraid we wouldn't end up all being friends," she confessed. "But, in fact, it's turned out the opposite. We're really good friends."

"You're all very different, but you have a lot in common."

"We so do," she said, laughing. "We all fell in love with seven very difficult men."

He chuckled. "That you did." He glanced around. "And now I can see why you were figuring out if there was enough room for a party here. With Levi and Ice coming in, things are kicking up. I'm wondering the same thing."

She walked out over the backyard. "If we have this all nicely mowed, and we set up tables, there should be plenty of room."

"Most people, if they're nicely dressed," he said, "will stick to the patio."

"Sure."

He turned to study the space up against the house. "But you're right. We could move all of that back out from underneath here, and people could stand around and talk. We could bring out more seating and have the tables—providing the weather forecast is any good—maybe out in the open air." He frowned. "It's the first time I've ever thought about doing any kind of formal entertaining here."

"I think seating will be a bit of an issue." She looked around. "It's possible others can bring some of their outdoor furniture. We might need to invest in some too."

He looked at her and walked over to the pool house. "You know? I believe we have a bunch more loungers. More than that, I think we have stackable chairs. Not enough for the party but maybe enough to set up a few seating areas. He unlocked the door to the pool house and stepped inside. Immediately Dotty wandered in to nose around.

Kat peered over his shoulder. "I've never even looked in

here," she exclaimed.

"No, it's not a place I come to unless there's a problem with the pool system. I keep all the chemicals in here, but, at the same time, it was always a good place to store the outdoor stuff." He brought out stacks of metal chairs. "These would give us some nice seating. Particularly if we have a few bistro tables."

"We can probably rent some stuff." She studied the chairs. "These just need a good wash."

He brought out four high tables.

She stared at them in surprise. "Those are perfect. That's like standing height. So, we can put platters of hors d'oeuvres on them, and people can rest a glass on them. The chairs can be set up in nice little clusters for little groups to sit at."

He brought out three more stacks.

"Okay, so that's what? We've got twenty chairs?"

"Twenty-four," he said, bringing out the last of them. "And I've got four of these tables." He returned to the small room. "And three smaller ones." He brought those out.

"Why do you have all of these?"

"It was my parents' home, remember?"

She nodded. "Still, this is a fair bit of outdoor furniture."

"It is, but my mom liked bargains. So, if they went to a garage sale and saw something in particular they wanted, they got it."

"Well, we can be thankful for your mom's foresight because this is perfect. This weekend maybe, when everybody comes over, we can discuss how we want to set up the backyard."

"We can do that." He glanced at her. "Are you okay to make it fancy dress?" He waited for her reaction, delighted to see a huge smile break across her face.

"I'm surprised you want to do something formal," Kat said. "But I'm really excited about the idea."

"Do you have a dress? Because, if I'm wearing a suit, it'd be nice to see you dressed up."

"I have a couple," she said with a big smile. "I have to check and see if I have shoes though." She stared down at her prosthetic leg and frowned. "I feel like I need to make a leg that has a built-in higher heel."

"Can you do that?"

She tossed him a cheeky grin. "I can do anything I want to do."

Laughter rumbled from his chest. "That is so true."

She waltzed into his arms. "What I'm really looking forward to is seeing you in a suit."

"I have a nice formal suit." He looked down at his long frame. "If it still fits. I haven't had an occasion to wear that one since my accident."

"Has your body shape changed that much?"

He shrugged. "Most of my other clothes still fit, so I presume it will. But an ill-fitting suit is way worse than no suit."

She frowned, thinking about it. "If you want to put it on, I can take a look. I'm sure we can always get a tailor to add a tuck and nip if you need it?"

"I'll see to it later," he compromised. He glanced around at his large backyard. "I guess it's a really good time to be happy about the size of the backyard."

"And the pool and the massive patio space," she said. "We can entertain forty in here easily."

"There won't be that many coming. But, as long as we've got twenty, we should be good."

"Sounds good to me." He had no clue the numbers

would be a little higher than he expected. She was looking at thirty-three guests plus the fourteen of them. She smiled, headed back into the kitchen and called out, "I presume we're barbecuing again?"

"Unless you want something else?"

"I'm totally okay with barbecue every night." She laughed. "Particularly if I don't have to do all the cooking."

"Nope. I'm happy to do my share." He walked toward the grill. "I guess we could always barbecue at the party?"

"Maybe. Can't say I'm particularly in love with the idea of you barbecuing in a suit though."

"Oh." He frowned. "I hadn't considered that."

"No problem, dear," she said cheerily. "That's why you have me."

"To remind me how silly I'd look barbecuing in a suit?" he asked with a grin, raising an eyebrow at her.

"Nope, not at all," she said, laughing. "But to point out things you never thought of."

He nodded. "I think that's called teamwork."

"Exactly. We're a hell of a team." She turned to look at him. "Right?"

He nodded and grinned. "The best."

CHAPTER 8

K AT PULLED UP in front of the restaurant. She hopped out to see Honey parking beside her within seconds. She watched Minx and Morning coming in too. The women were looking slightly more haggard. Every week it seemed like things were heating up, becoming that much more intense. More plans, more decisions to be made. Who would have thought planning a wedding could be so crazy? But they were planning seven. Seven *secret* weddings. Kat had to be nuts to have thought she could pull this off.

She walked in, her arm linked with Honey's, and headed to the room the restaurant always had ready for them. As they sat down, Hindy came over and asked if they wanted coffee. Kat shook her head. "I need a drink. White wine please. And thanks, Hindy, for helping us out with catering on such short notice."

She waved and she headed to the kitchen.

Honey chuckled. "Bad morning?"

"No." Something settled inside her at just being able to come together and talk to these women who had ended up becoming such good friends. She smiled as two more arrived and took their places. "Maybe just nerves."

Honey winced.

Hindy walked in then with a glass of white wine.

Honey said, "You better make that one for me too."

Laughter burbled up. Kat said with a big grin, "Nerves?"

"Oh, yeah. We're running out of time. And so many things we don't have lined up yet."

"I know," Kat said. "At times I think we should just call off the whole damn thing because we can't do a decent job."

"No, we can't do that," Morning said, her voice determined. "I know this is nuts. I know it's crazy. And I know we're putting the men on the spot. But I brought up the subject of marriage just weeks ago, and Geir was all about saying he didn't want to plan for the future because he still had more potential surgeries, and he didn't want the future to lock me down and all kinds of garbage. It made me so angry."

"Of course it did," Kat said. "And I think, to some extent, that's what the men are saying at every turn. I think they're afraid."

"You know every one of them would get angry if we even brought up such a possibility," Allison said. "They've come so damn far. They've survived so much, handled so much. And now that they're taking on jobs, doing security work and investigative work, forming their own company together, it's like they've got a new lease on life. But they're also petrified it won't work out for them. And anything else on their plate right now is just too much."

"I can agree with that," Faith said quietly. "It's hard to know when it's too much. But, every once in a while, they say something, and you kind of look at them sideways and think, I know where that's coming from."

"Exactly," Honey said. "I think we have to do this. We've already got so much in play, so much going on." She glanced at Kat with a reminder. "You didn't make it to the second fitting at the dressmaker's, did you?"

Kat groaned. "No, I had to cancel the appointment last week." She pulled out her day planner. "Look. I had a cancellation this afternoon, so maybe I can sneak it in there." She frowned, chewing the end of her pencil.

"The sooner, the better," Honey said. "We can do without a lot of things. But we really need the dresses."

Kat chuckled. "We could always wear bikinis. We'll be poolside anyway."

The women laughed. "I'm pretty sure the bikinis will come out later," Clary said.

Allison said, "We'll be so stressed, so worried, so tired, we're likely to strip off our wedding gowns and jump in."

"You know something? I don't think one of those men would argue." Kat quickly jotted down a note about the dressmaker, pulled out her phone and sent a text to her assistant. "I'll get Jim to call and see if he can get me squeezed in this afternoon."

"Does he know?"

"He knows and is being very helpful. He's assisting Marisa with the decorating," she muttered, staring down at the scrawled message that didn't seem to make any sense even though she wrote it herself. "I can't seem to read my own writing." She raised her gaze. "I've invited him too as he's so involved."

The others nodded. "Good. You're really close to him, aren't you?"

"Him and his partner. Oh, and I added Jim's partner to the guest list." She looked around at everyone else. "Anybody else fraying at the edges?"

"Are you kidding?" Clary said. "I came apart a long time ago."

That elicited a laugh from everyone.

Kat grinned at her. "You're always the coolest and collected of all."

Clary stared at her in shock. "That is so not true. Maybe I'm just better at hiding the frayed edges."

At that point Honey's wine was delivered.

Clary looked at it. "Hindy, why don't you give us all a round. We'll follow it up with coffee after our meal."

Hindy chuckled. "The date is coming up, isn't it?"

"Way too fast," Morning said. "I don't know that I'll be ready." She looked at the others. "I mean, we're talking in *days* now."

"Nineteen," Kat said, her voice somber, almost dark. "Nineteen days."

Silence fell as they all thought about everything that had to come together in those few days.

Faith said, "Did you touch base with Levi and Ice this last week?"

Kat nodded. "Levi has got the men playing their part. They all know Levi is supposed to ask Ice to marry him, so all the men will show up in black suits. Apparently they all have something that will do the job."

"I know Laszlo certainly does. It's beautiful. He tried it on the other day, and he looks really sharp," Minx said with a smile.

"Exactly. Badger still has to drop his off at the dry cleaners or the tailor's, depending"—she shook her head with a grin—"but, other than that, he is good to go." Kat said thoughtfully, "Our dresses are simple and elegant, and the men's black suits will be too. We'll look great."

"They probably all won't be the same color black though," Morning noted.

"Says our resident professional artist," Allison said with a smile.

"I don't think that matters so much," Kat said to Allison. "Our dresses aren't going to be exactly the same color white either. And the guys'll all have a different-colored tie, which we have to get." Her gaze swept around the room. "Unless anybody else handled that detail already?"

All the women shook their heads.

Kat sighed. "That's very important because we have to match each up to the flowers."

"I can ask the florist," Clary said. "I'm heading there this afternoon. They might at least give us sample colors so I can take them to a gentleman's store."

"I'll be devastated if I can't have that beautiful fuchsia," Minx said. "But I'd rather find out now because what I ideally want is us to match our husbands' apparel."

Just hearing that word *husband* made everybody stop. They turned to look at Minx.

She coyly murmured, "What? I was just trying out the word." She had a big grin on her face.

Hindy brought in a big tray, served a glass of wine to everyone and took their lunch orders.

"You realize we only have two more weeks to meet like this." Kat picked up her glass of wine and held it up. "To us and to a very happy Labor Day weekend."

Everyone held up their glasses and *clink*ed them together. "To our weddings."

Kat sipped from her glass, enjoying the cool feel as the wine hit her throat. She set it back down again. "Just over two weeks. Good God."

"We have to have more meetings," Honey stated. "Nineteen days only. And we need every one of those days."

"Anybody running into last-minute snags with their

schedules?" Allison asked.

"No, not yet," Minx said. "When I accepted my job, I told my new boss how I would need some time off on Labor Day weekend. So I should be able to avoid on-call duty."

"Honey, what about you?" Clary asked. "Any idea what you're doing for your schedule?"

"I'm not planning on having my honeymoon directly afterward," she said, "so I'm just taking off the long weekend. I'll be back to work on Tuesday."

Honey turned to look at Kat. "And you?"

"Same." Kat looked at Allison. "And you?"

Allison nodded. "I did bring it up in my interview. So I'll be getting the weekend off."

In mass everyone turned to look at Faith. She threw up her hands. "Hey, don't look at me. I promise I'll be there."

Everyone narrowed their gaze.

She sighed. "I've got Sunday and Monday off. Saturday was the issue."

The others winced. "That is *the* wedding day, remember?"

"I know. They had me doing a Hong Kong flight coming in first thing in the morning," she said. "I got it changed earlier today."

Clary asked, "Did we ever get somebody to do our hair?"

Honey pulled out her notepad. "Who was supposed to look into that? I have it down, but I didn't put somebody's name beside it."

"I talked to my hairdresser," Clary said. "She said she does do weddings. And, depending on how elaborate a style we want, she needs hours per person."

"And we're out of time."

Kat shook her head. "Let me send a text to mine. I know

she does beautiful hairdos. We don't need anything too elaborate, I don't think. At least I don't. But I do want my hair done." She sent off a text to her hairdresser and set her phone down. "She has at least three hair stylists that could do the job with her. It depends on their schedule." Her phone rang a moment later. She picked it up, took a look and said, "It's her." She put the phone to her ear. "Hey, Beth. I have an unexpected last-minute request. What's your schedule like for the Saturday of Labor Day weekend?" She listened and nodded. "Any chance you want to be booked to do seven heads?" She continued listening as the woman checked her calendar. "It's for a wedding."

Beth sighed. "Those take forever. I don't know that I can do that many at one time."

"Well, it's for seven of us. It can't be too fancy because ..." Kat raised her gaze, looking around at the women and whispered, "Do I tell her?"

Honey said, "You pretty well have to."

"Beth, this is a special circumstance. We'll be in normal clothes, and nobody'll really know what's going on until late afternoon, and then we're changing into our wedding dresses."

"Are you saying this is a surprise wedding?" Beth asked, her tone shocked. "All seven of you?"

"The wedding of a lifetime," Kat said in a wheedling tone. "We all want a somewhat elegant do but not too fancy." She looked around at the women, an eyebrow raised.

Everybody nodded. "And we have some with short hair, so I don't know how fancy it can be."

"I need head shots of everybody," Beth said. "And then I have to check out my availability. I'll get back to you."

"Okay, good. I'll send those photos right away." She

tossed back the rest of her white wine, stood and walked around, deliberately taking photos of everyone at the table. And then she turned her phone to take a selfie. She sent them all to Beth. "Anybody have any clue what you want for a hairstyle?"

The other women just stared at her.

"Jesus. I can't even imagine. I'm not interested in any of those big fancy dos," Clary said. "But maybe ringlets and flowers in my hair down one side."

"That's possible," Kat said. "You would wear something like that very well."

Clary shrugged. "It would go along with the flowers in my bouquet."

"If we're doing something like that, then we need extra flowers from the florist," Honey said.

The other women groaned.

"This is just getting more and more complicated."

"Only if we let it," Allison said firmly. "Look at all we've survived to get here. And considering how much we've already accomplished, I think we've done amazingly well." She glanced over at Morning. "What about food? Any idea where we're at?"

Morning nodded. "Alfred's bringing the desserts and a selection of savory items we can throw in an oven at Kat's place. Any of us could do that, in theory." She pulled her notepad toward her. "I don't know if you all want to know exactly what he's prepping for us. Most of it will be ready to serve. I believe he's coming up the day of the wedding."

Everyone turned to look at Kat for confirmation.

She nodded. "That's my understanding too. Levi and Ice are potentially coming on Friday night, and we are telling Badger that Alfred is staying at a friend's on Friday night and will arrive Saturday to handle the kitchen. Bailey is doing the baking at the compound, but Alfred is doing the delivery. Our lovely Hindy has arranged for several hot dishes and small finger foods for after the ceremony. To go along with cake, which will, of course, be a single large wedding cake not multiple birthday cakes. Plus there'll be hors d'oeuvres and appetizers."

"With lots of red meat for our men?" Allison asked in a drawling tone. "If they have that they may not miss having groom's cake."

Morning chuckled. "Yes, and there'll be some lighter fare for us ladies. And as long as they have lots of cake I think they won't care that some men order a groom's cake." She batted her eyes. "There'll be some seafood too," she added as an afterthought.

"Prawns, shrimp, scallops?" Faith asked hopefully.

Morning chuckled. "All of the above. And many puff pastry wraps and rolls."

"Sounds good. I'm totally happy to leave that to you to coordinate, Morning." Kat turned to look at Faith. "Were you the one doing the music?"

"Well, I've been trying to do the music. I think you're the one not responding to my questions."

Kat winced. "Sorry, it's hard to listen to it when I don't have anybody around me. I really would like to hear it in privacy."

Faith chuckled. "In that case, let me bring it up here." She opened her laptop and brought up the series. "We were going to play this set." She hit Play.

A melody Kat couldn't name came on, putting an instant smile on her face. "I love that song. But I can't even remember what it's called."

"It's one that all the rest of us have agreed on, as long as you're okay with it," Faith said. And she continued to go through the set, letting Kat hear the music.

"And what about at the actual wedding?"

"We thought we would do the traditional wedding march." She looked around. "Unless anybody has a reason not to."

"Let me think about that," Honey said. "It's not that I'm against it. But I'm thinking there has to be something a little better suited for us." Honey's fingers drummed on the table beside her plate. "Surely there's a song that speaks to everything we've come through."

"A song about catching you blindside?" Faith glanced around with a big grin on her face. "Everybody is still going forward, right? Because no way we can handle any one of us getting cold feet at this late date."

"No, no cold feet," Allison said. "Nervous feet, definitely chilled feet. But, no, none that will turn around and run in the opposite direction."

"You have to remember too," Clary said, "if any of us do get cold feet, that relationship is basically over because we'll have left him standing at the altar for his surprise wedding where everybody else will have a partner." Then her face brightened. "And I'd be very happy with the traditional wedding march."

Faith nodded. "I would too." She glanced around. "Anyone disagree?"

And just like that they had an agreement.

Feeling cheered, Kat asked, "Are the flowers all organized?"

"Except for the damn matching ties."

Kat nodded but frowned. They ran through a list of

what each person had to do. Then they sat back, exchanging glances.

"You know something?" Minx said. "We're damn close."

"I spoke to Marisa," Kat added. "She's got a justice of the peace. We've got the licenses to do."

"We have to get those," Honey stated. "Can't forget that."

"And she wants to decorate the backyard nicely." Kat frowned. "It'll be a little hard to do that and keep it not too wedding-ish."

Faith snorted. "I can't imagine how we're making any of this happen without it looking like a wedding."

"Right?" Kat checked her watch and groaned. "It seems like all I'm doing is running from thing to thing right now."

"That's okay. In another couple weeks, this will all be over," Allison said.

At that Faith froze, looked around at everybody and said, "Can you believe it? Can you believe what we're doing?"

The others looked at each other and then shrugged.

"You'll be standing strong on this, Kat, right?" Clary asked. "It was your idea after all."

Kat gave her a slow smile. "There's nothing I want more than to be married to Badger."

"Now let's just hope Badger wants to be married to you." Honey chuckled.

Kat rolled her eyes. "That is what keeps me awake at night."

Instantly silence settled.

"Do you really doubt he wants to?" Allison asked.

Kat shook her head slowly. "No, I believe it is what he truly wants. I don't believe he's anywhere close to ready to asking me. I think that would be, you know, maybe three, four, five, six, seven, eight, nine … I don't know, twenty years down the road before he thought he would ever be good enough, and he wouldn't want to be a burden to me. He somehow seems to think that, if we're not married, then I could pack up and leave because that's what I should do. He might be able to scare me off, but, once there's that commitment, it's a lifetime."

Minx nodded slowly. "The thing is, it *is* a lifetime."

Morning added, "It is a commitment. For me it's a lifetime commitment. And I can certainly see Geir saying the same thing. That, if we weren't married, he could chase me away, so I would go off and have a supposed better life. But there's just something about the commitment behind that piece of paper."

"Rings?" Honey asked urgently. "What about rings? We're out of time."

"I was thinking about that," Allison said. "We could just buy plain bands. And then it's up to the individual couples afterward if they want to have an engagement ring to go with it. Alternatively we could buy the wedding rings that have engagement rings as a set."

"We could also just have simple rings as stand-in rings, and then we can go shopping for the real rings afterward," Minx suggested. "I saw a really cute pair of handcuffs that were meant to be rings."

Everyone looked at her in shock.

Her laughter peeled across the room. "I'm joking about the handcuff rings. But I did see them. I'm not suggesting we do that. But sometimes—when the rings aren't ready, have to be resized, ordered in or are lost—any ring will do the job as it's just symbolic."

"I have another suggestion," Kat said. "Although they're

not terribly fancy."

The women looked at her with raised eyebrows.

"I was thinking about it earlier. I was going to bring it up, then forgot about it. Thought about it again and then decided you'd all want something much nicer."

"Speak up, girl," Honey said.

Kat took a deep breath. "The company I work with makes rings out of the same titanium I use to add support to the men's prosthetics." She dug in her purse, set it on her lap, opened up the photos she kept inside and passed them around. "They're simple, simple titanium rings, but these are braided with ivory, jade, gold, or however you want to mix it up. They're unisex and can be done in all sizes. I like them, but you may not." She shrugged. "It was just a thought."

Faith looked at her. "You know something? I think the men would like that. They are a rare breed, and are all connected to you, so displaying some of your artwork—your engineering—that's a perfect connection to their struggle, their survival. These men of steel would have a very personal reminder of our place in their lives."

Kat said quietly, "I'm really partial to the braided one with a small ivory rose in the center."

The women fell into a heavy discussion about the rings.

"This isn't something they do on a wide distribution," Kat added. "I just happened to ask them about it, and they sent me some of these as prototypes."

"So they're not mass-marketed? They're not something we'd be buying off a shelf?" Faith asked. "I like that they are so unique."

"What about sizing? Do we have time?" Honey asked.

Kat nodded. "Not only that, we could get them engraved. I've been talking to the manufacturer off and on for a week. He said Labor Day was doable. They would sit down for an afternoon with a designer and get them worked up."

Morning said, "I love this ivory one that's the reverse to the titanium one." She held it out.

They could see it was a matched set.

"Is that a butterfly in the center?" Honey asked.

Kat nodded. "Aren't they beautiful?"

"The thing is, they would be wedding rings. Not fancy engagement rings. No diamonds or jewels and no five thousand dollar price tag. They're not cheap, but they're each under five hundred. So, for a grand, we get matching rings for both of us."

"That's quite reasonable," Honey said.

Kat nodded. "We could also go cheaper yet again. But I think it would be important for each of us to have a design we really like. And one that we think the men will really like too."

"Exactly. The thing is, you notice they don't wear any jewelry. And they're not into anything ornate. They would want something simple."

"They would want something strong, something that represents union and strength." Faith studied the rings in the photos. "I have to admit. I have been looking online, and I've seen lots of diamond rings and emerald rings that I thought would be my preference, but"—she waved her hand—"they just don't appeal. The man I'm with is not of that world. Neither am I." She tapped the photo in front of her. "But honestly, I love these."

Kat nodded. "That's how I felt. They seemed so much more like what Badger would want. They're simple. They're elegant, yet they're masculine. And, more than that, they're a symbol of strength for somebody who surmounted incredible odds to be where he is today."

"Exactly," Allison said, looking at the rings. "And lots of designs are here. You know? I wouldn't mind having this one myself." She tapped a matching set. "I think this is jade, isn't it?"

"I think it's inlaid with jade pieces, yes," Kat said. "These designs have all been created, each unique. But we can make slight tweaks so they're ours." She glanced down at her watch. "Dammit. I've got to run again. Keep these. I've got more at home. If you want, I can send them to you by email. But, if this is what we want to do, we have to decide fast."

With a quick glance at the others, she waved and took off. One of these days, she would be able to sit and relax and have lunch with the girls. But it seemed like they came in with a million questions and had to run with a million more.

Back at the office, her assistant was grinning as he met her at the front desk on the way to her office. "Well, you ready?"

"It seems like, not only am I *not* ready but I'm getting further behind," she fretted. "How is it that a wedding can take so much time to get through?"

"Oh, the wedding itself will be like five minutes," he said with a chuckle. "But all the details, now that's where it counts." He glanced at his calendar. "Marisa needs you to make a bunch of decisions on the decorating."

She stopped in her tracks and groaned. "Oh, my God. I forgot about that. But I do have to go to the dressmaker's. Maybe I can meet Marisa afterward?" She frowned. "I could always meet her for drinks somewhere and go over stuff. I can't have her come to the house, not without raising suspicions." She nodded, as if that was decided. "Do you really think this isn't over-the-top? I mean, a little bit of decoration, but we can't have too much?"

"Not at all," her assistant said with a wave of his hand. "We'll come in and set up ten tables. Next thing you know, it'll be done and fixed up nice, while you guys are still standing around taking pictures."

"Pictures!" she cried, her face paling. "Oh, my God. I forgot a photographer." She stared at him in a panic. "It's only a couple weeks away."

He looked at her. "Wasn't somebody supposed to do that?"

She thought so, but, at the same time, she couldn't remember. "I'll contact Honey because we do need photographs." She marched into her office, plunked her butt down behind her desk and sent Honey a quick text.

By then her assistant was at the door, saying, "Mrs. Marshall is here for you."

She sighed and put it all to the back of her mind. With a determined smile, she plastered a bright welcoming look on her face and stood to greet her next patient.

BADGER WANDERED THE backyard. The rest of his unit was all here. "She's got some kind of a planner. Something like a party planner or event planner. I didn't want to get very fancy, but I don't know how to tell Kat to keep it low-key."

"If she makes it too fancy, Ice will get suspicious," Erick said as he walked beside his friend.

They both held beers, kind of a celebration after coming away from the lawyer's office triumphant, and yet a little warier, having gone through the steps of incorporating their business. They'd all signed on as equal partners, and, as much as it was a daunting thought, it was also a brand-new beginning. They had all decided to come to Badger's for a beer and to celebrate. But, once the discussion came up about how many people would be here for Labor Day weekend, the topic turned to the outdoor space and how to decorate it.

"Well, you'd think that an event planner would come in with lights, make it look nice for the afternoon and evening, and the next morning it can all go away." Badger laughed. "What do I know? I've been to funerals, and I've been to a couple weddings. But they were pretty big fancy deals. An engagement party, I have no clue."

"Right?" Laszlo said from beside them. He looked at the large expanse of grass. "If this is nicely trimmed, we can have a lot of people out here."

"Do you think it's safe with it being grass?"

Laszlo nodded. "It'll be fine, providing the weather is good. Did you consider what you'll do if the weather is lousy?"

Badger groaned. "If it's lousy, I can hold a mess of people inside. Unless we want to be outside and put up cabanas. But I sure wouldn't want to if we didn't need to."

"Did you get a menu from Kat yet?"

Badger shook his head and groaned. "No. Every time I broach it, she gets all flustered and clams up. I can't tell if she's stressed about making too much of these plans or if she's thinking I'll get upset because she either hasn't planned enough or has planned too much."

"As long as there's lots of good food, I don't care." Talon walked out of the kitchen door, a cold beer in his hand. "That's what she has to remember. People need food. And not just girly food."

"What's girly food?"

The men snickered.

"Those little tiny things you can't pick up and eat. They're like ready-to-pop-in-your-mouth one-bite foods. Or veggie platters," Talon said with a snarl. "I mean, I don't mind sliders. At least they are burgers. But I really don't want little tiny canapés or fluffy things. And I definitely don't want little tiny desserts that won't taste like anything."

"Okay, you guys are scaring me," Badger said. "I didn't put any thought into that."

"We have to trust in Kat."

"Not only trust in Kat," Badger said, "we have to treat her well, and we have to like whatever it is she's done because she's gone to a ton of effort over this."

"I think she's involved Honey too because I see Honey always with a notepad, jotting down stuff, crossing off stuff, making phone calls, sending emails. I asked her a couple times what she was up to, and she said she was helping Kat."

"Right, that's the same for Allison. She said she was meeting the girls for lunch to discuss a few things with them."

"And yet they don't know about the real reason for the formal party, right?"

The men all shook their heads.

"No, they just think it's a nice weekend bash."

Badger nodded with relief. "Because that was the one thing Levi wanted to make sure of, that the women didn't know," he warned. "You know that, as soon as one of them knows, they'll all know."

"You got to make sure there's beer here, Badger," Erick said. "I'll have a glass of champagne and toast with the rest of you, but you know I'd really rather have a beer."

"So would I," Cade said. "It'll be funny enough to be in a suit again."

"I'm kind of looking forward to it," Laszlo said. "I want to wear my suit to something other than a funeral for a change."

That silenced them all.

"Do you think it's okay to wear a black suit for this thing?" Geir asked. "It never occurred to me to wear anything different."

He watched as relief washed over the men's faces.

"Don't forget it's not us on display," Badger said. "This is all to help support Levi. It's important to him. He's done a lot for us."

Erick said, "Not a problem. If Levi needs this from us, we're happy to help."

Badger smiled. "I can't wait to see Ice's face."

"Right, she must think he's never going to ask her."

"Badger, did Levi tell you when he would do this? Like at dusk or whenever, so we know when to pay attention?" Erick asked.

Badger shook his head. "Levi said he'd wing it, when he felt the time was right."

"Have any of you considered this whole event?" Erick asked, a note of humor in his voice. "I mean, all this preparation for Levi to pop the question. What the hell? Since when is that a thing?"

That started a heavy discussion about the trend in engagements, the old-fashioned route versus new social media and parties.

Badger thought all of it was garbage. "Isn't it just better to find a quiet time and ask her in privacy, where she can say yes or no?"

"If I was ready to ask Morning, I wouldn't be asking her anyplace where she has an option to say no," Geir said in surprise. "No way in hell I want to face rejection at that point."

And that sent the men off yet again.

"That makes sense," Badger muttered. He walked to his lounger and sat down, looking out at the yard, envisioning it lit up with nice lights, and everyone formally dressed, and he smiled. "I wonder if Levi thought about photographs."

The guys took one look at him, and Talon said, "No idea. We don't really need a photographer, do we?"

Badger shrugged. "Maybe. But, if Kat is dressed up, I want a picture of her."

The others grinned.

"Right. Do we know a photographer?" Cade asked.

They all shook their heads.

"We're not slouches in that department," Badger said, "but neither are we professional photographers."

"I think you mean engagement-party photographers," Erick joked. "I still think the whole thing is over-the-top."

"Yeah, but you know something? Women love over-the-top," Laszlo said.

Erick shook his head. "There's over-the-top, and then there's over-the-top," he exclaimed.

That had all the men talking yet again.

Finally Cade looked at his watch and said, "I can tell you one thing. We'll all be in deep shit if we're not heading home soon."

Badger checked his watch and realized it was six already. "I wonder where Kat is."

The men pulled out their phones.

"None of the women have contacted us."

They shook their heads. But they all made their way to the front door and disappeared.

As soon as they were gone, Badger picked up his phone and called Kat. When she answered on the second ring, her voice sounded distracted. He said, "Kat, you okay?"

She groaned. "I am. I'm just here with Marisa, trying to get the last of the details hammered out for the party."

"It's still a couple weeks away, honey. We have time."

"I know. I'll be home in another hour."

He smiled. "No problem. Are you eating dinner there?"

"Yeah, I am. Sorry. I should have said something."

"Not an issue." He put away his phone, walked into the kitchen and pulled out leftover salads and served himself.

Holding the plate, he wandered around the lower floor of his house, Dotty keeping pace with his footsteps, figuring out just what they should do if they ended up with, like, forty people inside. He could handle twenty easily, but forty trying to stay out of the rain might be a bit much.

Just as he finished eating, his phone rang. He glanced down to see it was Ice. He lifted the phone to his ear. "Hey, Ice. What's up?"

"Do you happen to have an extra room Saturday night? Alfred is coming with us but will be staying at a friend's on Friday night," Ice said, fatigue in her voice. "But he doesn't have a place to stay for the second night."

"Sure, no problem," Badger said. "Ice, you sound tired."

"Yeah," she said. "Just really busy right now. And Levi seems to be a little more distracted than usual."

It was all Badger could do to keep his mouth shut. But he ended the call with a big grin. He held up his beer in a cheer to Levi and said, "Man, have you ever set something in motion."

And he popped the top and took a big long drink.

CHAPTER 9

THE FOLLOWING WEEK Kat sat down at the restaurant. This time she was the first one in. She had her notepad out, going over her list. She'd been to the dressmaker. Check. She'd been to the florist. Check. She had a tie for Badger. Check. She'd gone over all the final details with Marisa. Check. Jim had taken a huge list of details for him and Marisa to handle. Later. She was more or less feeling in control.

When Hindy walked in with a surprised look on her face, Kat asked, "What's up, Hindy?"

"You're a day early."

Kat stared at her in shock. "Today is Tuesday, right?"

Hindy shook her head. "Today is Monday, honey."

Kat groaned and sat back. "But, hey, I was just checking things off and feeling really good about everything, and now I realize I'm a full day early." She smiled, followed by a heavy sigh. "Well, since I'm here anyway, will you bring me a salad and a coffee? I'll keep working away."

With a big grin, Hindy turned and walked away.

Kat picked up the phone and called Honey. "Guess where I am?"

"At the restaurant?"

"How did you know?"

"Because I was about to head there myself, and I realized

it was the wrong day."

"Well, come anyway," Kat said. "Because I'm sitting in the room all alone, feeling like an idiot."

Honey laughed. "Okay, I'll be there in five."

By the time her friend arrived, Kat had ordered coffee for both of them.

As they compared lists, Honey said, "You know we're really close."

Kat nodded. "I even got in the ring orders for everybody. Of course we'll need to pick them up the day before. They'll need every day to get them all done by then."

"I know. We left that part to the last minute. Another thing that was worrying me," Honey said. "Our hair. Did we ever get that locked down?"

Kat nodded. "We have three hairdressers coming in that day. Which means, somehow, I have to hide that from Badger."

Honey nodded. "It's a problem for all of us, but we could do some of it at my house and some of it potentially at someone else's, and we just all meet at your place at the right time, with our hair done."

"But we're supposed to all be together that day, completely dressed up, and, when it's time, go get changed and still have our hair looking gorgeous. And we need our makeup retouched. And then we're supposed to come out, right?"

That started a discussion about logistics and timing.

Honey sat back with a groan a good half-hour later. "This is why there are rehearsals."

Kat chuckled. "Like we'll get a chance to do that."

"We could try at my house," Honey said, "but we need a reason to get rid of Erick because we really do need a chance to figure out how the timing will work. We can't have the men know ahead of time."

Kat thought about it. "We only have this weekend. The following weekend is the wedding."

"And we'll need every day this week and this weekend to make this work."

Kat nodded. "I don't think I can wait until the final day."

"Why don't we take off Friday afternoon before the wedding? Have everybody meet at my place, and we'll go through a logistics rehearsal."

"That might work," Kat said thoughtfully. "Levi and Ice are coming Friday evening. So, we'll have a social time with them, and then Saturday I think they said they were doing some running around. The party is supposed to start at what, three? And then the wedding itself starts at seven?"

"That all works," Honey said. "I've got the additional tables and dishes being delivered early. They couldn't come later, so the delivery is set for eight-thirty that morning."

"It's a bit early," Kat said, frowning, "but at least we'll have it all for when we're ready."

"It has to work," Honey said. "The supply company was pretty adamant about the time frame. They're really behind on so much because it was very short notice."

"True enough," Kat said. "But we also have Alfred coming early on Saturday."

"Right."

They sat there for a long moment. Kat shuffled back in her chair and looked over at Honey. "Second thoughts?"

Honey shook her head. "No. This is what I really want. But I do have misgivings about forcing them into this."

Kat nodded. "My thoughts exactly."

"But I won't dare quit," Honey said, "because I think that would be devastating to everyone. We've all done this. We've all come this far. We've made such great plans. We've got a huge outlay on expenses. No way we can back out now."

"No, but we need to make sure absolutely nothing goes wrong right up to the last moment." Kat wondered if it was possible to even get through the next twelve days. As it was, her work schedule was steady, and the weekend was crammed with shopping, cleaning, rearranging furniture so there was more space inside and out.

BY THE TIME Friday's rehearsal rolled around, Kat was beside herself with nerves. She hadn't told Badger she'd taken the afternoon off because, if he thought she wasn't working, he would assume she would be home cleaning out the kitchen, getting ready for company. Instead, she was over at Honey's.

Since Badger had roped Erick into doing something, he wouldn't be home.

Kat walked in with a box in her hand at the same time Allison walked in with an envelope. Kat looked at the envelope and said, "Licenses?"

Allison nodded. "All the paperwork is in order. Everybody's paid up in full." She looked at the box and said, "OMG! Is that rings?"

Inside the kitchen all the women were busy discussing what they had. They had a collection of ties all in the right colors they would give to Ice to distribute. Or to Levi. They had to be labeled so he'd know exactly which man got which color too because that would be a disaster if the guys all ended up with the wrong colors. The boutonnieres and wedding bouquets were to be delivered Saturday afternoon. Ice was in charge of intercepting that delivery before any of the guys saw it. The catering was all lined up.

The women were a mess. Honey had champagne sitting open on the counter, and the glasses were flowing freely. Honey said, "I still can't believe we're doing this."

"Not only are we doing it but it's tomorrow. You all realize we're getting married tomorrow? This is our bachelorette party," Faith said with a big chuckle. She lifted her glass. "To us."

The ladies all raised their glasses, *clink*ed them together and took a drink.

Kat looked around the room. "How are we supposed to do a rehearsal?"

"This way." Honey opened the back door, and they stepped out into the yard. "This is approximately the backyard space beside the pool that you have. What I figure is, we'll get the men to stand over on the far side, each with a different colored tie. Ice and Levi will be our witnesses."

Kat groaned. "I forgot about that."

"So, once all the men are lined up, Ice will stand at the glass door to give us the heads-up, and then we'll all come outside. As the wedding march plays, we'll cross the lawn toward our men. And then we'll slip an arm through theirs, turning to face the justice of the peace all at once."

"And do we really think the men will just stand there, like robots, and let us do that?" Allison laughed.

The others shrieked in laughter.

"I can just imagine the expressions on their faces," Minx said. "First, they have to get over the shock of what they see.

Second, they have to get over the shock of what's happening. Hopefully by then, we can get the justice of the peace to ask the questions," Minx said. "But, no, I can't imagine this will go smoothly. There will be some hiccup."

The women stared at each other, each face showing the fear of rejection and the possible damage they could do to their relationships.

"I refuse to believe that," Kat said quietly. "I'm going through with this. I need to. It's the only way I'll feel like Badger will take this step."

The others nodded.

"But that doesn't mean I'll sleep tonight," Honey said. "I feel like I have to ask Erick's forgiveness in case I do something tomorrow he doesn't like."

The others frowned, but Kat understood. "You do what you need to do. But you show up on time." She glanced around at them. "We have three hairdressers at three different houses. Eight of us are getting our hair done, that includes Ice, just because she's a part of this. I think that long platinum braid of hers will look absolutely stunning if it goes up."

The others all agreed.

"Makeup. We'll touch up just before the wedding, and we'll all get changed in my room. All the dresses are currently in my spare room," Kat said. "They're all in dress bags, so …" Her voice trailed off as she was lost in thought. "Are we done?" She frowned. "It almost feels like we're done."

The women looked at each other.

Honey walked over and wrapped her arms around Kat, hugging her gently before stepping back. "For better or for worse, I'm really glad you put this in motion."

"I hope so because, if anything goes wrong, it could

mean the end to some beautiful friendships," she muttered.

Minx walked over and hugged her next. "But it's not your fault. We all came to this step on our own terms. It's what we all want."

Clary walked over, looping her arm through Kat's. "And we have to trust that the men know we're doing this for the right reasons."

"And of course," Minx said, laughing, "Levi and Ice appear to be having a ball with all of this."

"Oh, my God! It's so true." Kat groaned. She gave each one a hug. "Tomorrow. Remember we start at one o'clock for hair. Everybody's to convene at my place at three, correct?" With that note she gave a finger wave and walked out. As she stepped out the front door, she raised her face to the late-afternoon sun and sighed. "Please, please make this all go off without a hitch."

And she headed home.

BADGER AND KAT had had a hell of a night with Levi and Ice. Yet Kat had been on edge, and, no matter what he'd done, he couldn't seem to get her to relax. The next morning, Badger got out of bed, had a quick shower and walked downstairs. As he headed down the hallway, he saw Levi and Ice, sitting outside on the loungers. He walked onto the patio and said, "Nice to see early birds."

His guests smiled up at him. "We've always been early birds," Levi said, his voice low. "It's pretty hard to change the habits of a lifetime now."

Badger understood. "I'll put on the coffee and come back out." He walked into the kitchen, started the coffee, checked the fridge for breakfast supplies and realized it was completely stuffed for the party tonight. He shook his head. "Kat, you better get your ass out of bed soon," he muttered. But he was joking. He just hadn't a clue what he was supposed to serve for breakfast. Every shelf was so damn full.

When the coffee was done, he filled a tray with the carafe and cups, and took it outside, putting it on the small table. "You said Alfred was coming in today?"

Levi nodded. "He stayed with friends last night, but they're heading out of town today, so he was looking for a chance to come and stay with us until we go back home again."

"We're more than happy to have him," Badger said. "It's always good to have friends around."

As they sat here drinking coffee, Ice said, "Have you got any plans for today?"

Badger caught Levi's gaze and the tiny head shake that meant *don't tell her anything.* Badger smiled and said, "A little bit of shopping, maybe some errand running, not too sure yet. What about you?"

She smiled. "Early afternoon I'm getting my hair done." She slid a sideways glance at Levi. "Apparently there's a party tonight that's supposed to be pretty high-end. This guy here made me bring a dress I have yet to wear. He bought it for me a long time ago. It's not exactly something I can wear very often."

"I'm sure you'll look delightful in it," Badger said easily.

She rolled her eyes at him. "Maybe. It still won't be all that comfortable if I'm not dressed the way I am for work."

"It's good for you," Levi said. "Not everything is about work."

She chuckled. "No, it isn't. But, at the moment, we're

still waiting on the cement trucks to come and pour the new pool," she said in excitement. "I was thrilled to find out you had a pool here."

"And I hope you brought a bathing suit," Badger said. "Feel free to use the pool whenever."

She nodded. "If you don't mind, I'll change and get in some laps."

"Go for it," he said in surprise. "I'm sorry you felt you had to ask. You could have just gone in at five o'clock in the morning. I wouldn't have known."

She grinned. "Maybe I'll do that tomorrow morning." She got up and left.

They could hear her footsteps crossing the living room and hall floor to the bottom of the stairs, and then the creaks as she headed up.

Levi asked in a low voice, "Hey, are you guys ready?"

"I think so. Did you bring booze?"

"Alfred is bringing a bunch of it," Levi said. "We brought two vehicles. He's got one fully loaded with booze."

"Perfect," Badger said with satisfaction. "I was afraid we would have to make a trip to a couple liquor stores today."

"We may have to anyway," Levi said easily. "Did you even think about dishes and all that stuff?"

Badger winced. "You can bet I didn't. But I sure hope Kat did. If not, then I guess we have a few things to pick up this morning." He nodded, got up and refilled their coffee. As he was carrying the cups outside, Ice came downstairs in a bikini with a beach rap over her shoulders.

Long and lean, slim, muscled like a dancer, she walked past him with grace in every movement. With her hair in a long braid, she dropped the cover-up, walked to the end of the pool and dove in with a clean motion. Badger appreciated the strength and the agility as she swam from one end to the other. "She's a good swimmer," he said.

"Swim team," Levi said. "She's been bugging me for a pool since forever."

"I can see why." He looked up to see a very tousled Kat in the doorway. She covered her mouth to smother a yawn and smiled. "I see Ice is enjoying the pool." She walked over and took the spot where Ice had been sitting. "Good morning, Levi. How are you?"

He chuckled softly. "I'm fine. How are you?"

She beamed at him. "I'll be much better when I wake up. I've had a hard time sleeping this last week."

Badger frowned. "You didn't have a good night again, did you?"

She shook her head and smiled. "That's okay. I'll sleep much better tonight."

"I'm sorry the party caused you such stress," Badger said. "I didn't want you to knock yourself out over it."

She chuckled softly. "Some things are worth knocking ourselves out about." She caught Levi's grin.

Badger didn't quite understand what the look was about, but he was prepared for the undercurrents that had a ton of different meanings, given the secret party tonight. He turned toward Kat. "I was looking in the fridge, seeing what could be for breakfast. But it's jam-packed with food for tonight."

She laughed. "It so is. So is Honey's fridge. We are having a party, so we decided to make it a little more special."

"We won't need that much food," he said. "Surely?"

"If not," she countered, "we'll need it for the rest of the weekend anyway."

He shrugged at that. "That's probably true," he said. "But I didn't know what I was supposed to pull out for breakfast because I didn't know if some of that food was slotted for another dish."

"After I've had a couple cups of coffee, I'll start breakfast," she declared. She looked around. "I have a lot of running around to do and then appointments early this afternoon. Everybody's supposed to be here by three. So it'll be a busy day."

Badger wanted to ask more questions, but just then Ice hopped out of the pool and came over, dripping wet. She wrapped a towel around her hair and another around her body as she sat down in the morning sun. "Good morning, Kat," she exclaimed.

Kat looked over at her and smiled. "Nice to see you so bright and cheerful this morning," she teased.

Ice chuckled. "Hey, it's a beautiful day. I'm not at home. I'm not working. Everything is calm in our world. So it's a great time to come and visit."

After that, small talk resumed until Badger watched as Kat got up and headed into the kitchen. As she stepped in through the French doors, he called out, "Can I help?"

She tossed him a saucy grin. "I'm good," and she headed in.

Levi looked over at him. "You appear to be a man in love."

Badger smiled. "I am," he admitted. "And happy about it."

"That's the way it should be," Ice said with a gentle smile. "Relationships can be hard when you don't know where they're going and when you don't know how you feel."

"I have a good idea where I'm going, and I know exactly how I feel," Badger declared.

He wasn't sure if something extra was in their gazes, but, considering what Levi had planned for tonight at the party and that Ice had no clue, it just made this weekend all the more interesting. Badger was really enjoying the secrecy behind this mess. There was a lot of joy to be had tonight. He couldn't wait.

CHAPTER 10

B Y THE TIME one o'clock came around, Kat walked into Erick's house. As she entered the living room, Honey was there, smiling.

"Erick's gone. Badger needed his help," Honey said. "I think the men had to go for more booze or something or other," Honey said, waving her hand. "I feel like we'll be so full and so drunk, we won't care what else happens."

"Ice is at my house, waiting for Marisa and Jim, who are decorating."

Chuckling, the women walked in to the master bedroom where the hairstylist was setting up. "We have deliveries coming all afternoon. I had to get the men out of there," Kat exclaimed. "Ice is holding down the fort, accepting deliveries, putting everything into the spare room. We've got Alfred coming alone today, as he and Bailey decided she'd stay back there and look after those at the compound. As soon as he arrives, Ice will be freed up to get her hair done," she fretted.

"You're getting done first," Honey said, "and you can go back to take care of things. Our stylist will come over and do any final tweaks before the ceremony."

Obediently Kat sat down and let the hairstylist go to work. As she sat there with her eyes closed, her mind raced as she thought about all the things that had to come together. And they were down to the wire. Only a few more hours now before the wedding ceremony started, promptly at seven. That was in less than six hours. And she just couldn't imagine how much time she needed to get everything done on her list.

When the stylist gently patted her on the shoulders and said she could look, Kat's eyes flew open, and she gasped. Her hair was piled in ringlets off to the side, and her face … It had been done with soft makeup matching her natural skin tones but emphasizing the beauty she rarely saw in the mirror. "Wow."

Honey nodded. "We'll touch up the hair with the flowers later."

Kat hopped off the chair, studying her face in awe. "Wow, you've worked magic." She turned to Eloise, the hair stylist, who was blushing. Kat gave her a quick hug and said, "Thank you, thank you, thank you."

Eloise shrugged. "You're a beautiful woman. It's so much easier to work with someone who has great bones to begin with."

Honey gave Kat a big hug and said, "Come on. My turn. It's already two o'clock."

Kat stared at her in horror. "Oh, my God. I've got to go." And she bolted out the door and headed home. Back at the house she looked in the mirror again, realizing her hairstyle still held.

Ice took one look and whistled. "Wow."

"I know, right? That girl is magic." As she and Ice walked through to the kitchen, Kat realized Marisa was already out there.

Marisa waved and told her, "Go do your thing. Jim is here. We got this handled."

"Okay, but it's after two," Kat reminded them.

Marisa nodded. "Like I said, we got this."

Kat raced upstairs, with Ice at her heels. "Did everything arrive?" She walked into the spare room she had designated for the change room to see seven gown bags hanging in the closet. On the bed were seven florist's boxes, and all the matching ties were lined up nearby. She stared at it in awe. "Oh, my God! What are we doing here?"

"I think what you're doing is absolutely fantastic," Ice said. "And I wouldn't be helping you if I didn't think it was the right thing to do."

Tears sprang to Kat's eyes. She shook her head as she wiped them away gently, trying not to spoil her makeup. "I'm just such an emotional wreck right now."

Ice smiled. "So you should be. It's your wedding day."

Kat stopped in her tracks. She stared at Ice. "So it is." She motioned at Ice. "You need to go get your hair done. I'm fine here."

By the time three o'clock rolled around, nobody was here. Kat groaned as she stared at all the food and thought of the stuff not done. But Alfred was incredibly efficient.

He motioned her out of the kitchen. "I think I hear a vehicle now."

Kat picked up the pace and raced, slipping up the stairs and around the corner as she heard Badger coming in. She ran into the master bedroom, grabbed the clothes she needed and headed to the bathroom where she closed and locked the door.

There she stood for a long moment, studying the woman in the mirror. "I can't believe I did this," she whispered. She closed her eyes with her hands against her heart and just hugged herself for a moment. She needed this to go well. She so badly needed this to go well.

Realizing she heard Badger outside the door, she quickly stripped down and brought out the party dress she'd bought. It was more of a sheath style, simple, clean, with a slit up the one leg, and she realized she hadn't brought her dressy prosthetic in with her. It was definitely required for this outfit.

The dress was simple, a geometric mix of black and midnight blue with a jagged slash down the center of turquoise. It matched her makeup and everything. As she straightened up, she put on fresh deodorant and a spritz of perfume, and then she opened the door and walked out. Thankfully Badger wasn't there.

She crossed to the closet and pulled out her dressy prosthetic leg. Sitting down on the bed, she quickly switched into her dressy leg and stood. Then she walked to the mirror, took a final look and sighed. "Well, Kat, if nothing else, you look beautiful."

She opened the door and proceeded to the stairs. She could hear lots of noise and presumed people had begun to arrive.

As she got to the bottom of the staircase, Honey and Erick came in the door. Honey took one look and whistled. "Don't you look divine?"

Kat chuckled. "I could say the same for you."

The two women hooked arms and walked through to the kitchen. Badger was busy popping tops on beer for everyone as they came through, heading to the backyard. He took one look and stopped; the smile on his face was worth everything. He gave her a once-over, walked toward her, leaned down and kissed her hard. The kiss was possessive and hot.

By the time she sagged against him, he stepped back,

took one look at her face and said, "Now that's exactly the look I needed to see."

"And what look is that?" she asked, her lips tremulous.

"Well-loved," he said in a teasing manner.

Hot color rose over her face. She shot him a look, and he chuckled.

She walked out the back door to mingle, but her stomach was roiling with nerves. People arrived in waves. Some she'd met; some she hadn't. Dennis was here with his wife and little kids. She stopped to speak with him for a moment, then moved on to everyone else.

Badger grabbed her and said, "It's almost like everybody knows something's going on."

She looked at him. "Well, it's hardly a surprise birthday party, what with five of seven SEALs born in August and September gathered here today."

He nodded. "We need to get out some food. People are hungry with only snacks so far."

She then realized it was well past five. She took a deep breath, nodded and walked into the kitchen. There she found Alfred, already working on the food. Jim and his partner walked past, each carrying a large tray.

Jim winked at her.

She deliberately didn't say anything, just kept on walking. After conversing with Alfred and realizing all was handled, she took a deep breath and tried to relax. Time raced by.

Just then, Morning stepped up beside her. "Are you ready for this?"

She shook her head. "I'm so not."

They stopped at the glass doors and surveyed the noise and chaos outside. Music played; people talked. The three little kids were in the pool, but always somebody was there to watch them.

"This is definitely more of a big family barbecue party."

"It'll change once the sun goes down," Morning said.

Kat took a deep breath. "It'll change a lot very soon." She glanced around. "Looks like the men are disappearing."

"Good." Morning nodded. "We have a lot to get ready for in the next hour too."

"Some of the women have already started." Panic grabbed Kat by the throat, and she stood there for a long moment, incapable of moving.

Ice finally stepped up to her. "Go. It's late already. You need to go."

Kat shot her a panicked look. "I don't think I can."

Ice reached out, gripped Kat's fingers hard and said, "Kat, this is the moment you've been waiting for. Be strong. You know why you're doing this."

Kat nodded. "But what if it's not fair to him?"

The smile Ice gave her was full of sweetness and light and understanding. "Do you love him?"

She smiled. "With all my heart."

"Then do this. It's exactly what Badger needs."

Kat nodded once and disappeared. She wasn't sure she was convinced, but she knew the effort she'd put in wasn't something she would ignore now. Besides, six women were counting on her. Kat made it into the spare bedroom and stopped, seeing the women in various stages of dress— wedding dresses, bouquets, touching up makeup, adding flowers to their hair.

She clasped a hand to her mouth. "Oh, my God! You guys are so beautiful!"

The hairstylist was working on Minx, refreshing her hair,

adding flowers. She worked patiently and efficiently.

"I think we're going to be late," Honey fussed.

"I'm not even close to being ready," Kat cried out. She stepped out of her clothes and reached for her wedding dress. She had on brand-new lingerie underneath, and she gently worked her way into her wedding dress, exactly the same as the other women and yet unique to her. She stood in front of the mirror and sighed. "I can't believe we're doing this."

"Does everybody have their rings?"

"I believe Levi has them all."

A knock came on the door, and silence fell inside the room. Ice called through the door, "Kat, it's me. May I come in?"

Kat walked over and opened the door, letting Ice in.

Ice took one look, and tears came to her eyes. "Oh, my goodness," she cried softly, looking stunning herself in a gold sheath, her hair in long loose curls.

Kat hurriedly closed the door behind her. "I know, right?" She turned and asked Ice, "Can you zip me up please?"

Ice zipped up Kat and the other women. And true enough, they were late. It was past seven o'clock when Ice said, "I have to go down."

"Don't the men look gorgeous?" Kat whispered. "I can't believe how debonair they look."

Ice chuckled. "They sure do. Every one of them has a different-colored tie as instructed."

"I just hope they have the right ties," Kat said. "We really want to match our men."

Ice's laughter trailed all the way down the stairs.

Then it was Kat's turn to get her hair spruced up.

And finally they stood, all seven women staring at each

other.

The moment of truth.

The moment they'd been planning for, for weeks and weeks, stared at them.

"How do we make sure all the guests are outside so nobody sees us come down the stairs?"

Kat opened the door and stepped out. There was Alfred at the top of the stairs. He stopped, took one look and smiled. "Now this is a sight for sore eyes," he said.

"Alfred, is there any way to know if all the guests are outside?"

He nodded. "Jim and I and Marisa already did a full sweep. All are waiting for you ladies now."

They all slipped down the stairs, moving carefully in their wedding finery.

At the bottom of the stairs they stood in a circle around Alfred. He was just awestruck. Tears were in his eyes as he said, "I've never seen such a bevy of beautiful women."

They laughed; nervous twitters raced around the circle.

"We're barely able to make that walk outside right now," Kat said. "It's bad enough to be nervous when your groom expects you. But to think seven men are out there with no clue …"

Alfred gave a huge proud grin. "And not one of them will be upset either," he said. "We have photographers. Levi is busy talking to the men. As soon as I give the word, Levi will line them up so they're facing the glass doors. They will be standing off to the side. You'll like the little altar Marisa put together, and the justice of the peace is standing there, mingling with the rest."

"Right," Kat said. She nodded, firmed up her chin and said, "Let's do this."

Alfred reached out, patted her hand and said, "Yes." He walked ahead to the glass door.

She peered around the living room as he gave the motion to Levi who spread the men slightly apart. The justice of the peace who had been standing behind Levi listened to something Levi said, nodded, then stood waiting in front of the altar. The men couldn't see him because he was behind them.

The guests all realized something was happening. There were murmurs and cries and whispers. And then the music started to play. Nobody spoke a word.

Kat looked at the others and said, "That's our tune."

The women nodded to each other. Each reached out a hand, grabbed each other and said together, "We're doing this because we love them." They released their hands, and Kat, knowing she had to lead the way, walked through the living room and out the glass doors.

Instantly there were cries of surprise. But, as every woman came out—one, two, three, four, five, six, and finally Allison as the seventh—they stopped, bouquets in hand, on one side of the lawn across from the men in their wedding finery, staring at them across the way, and then slowly, one at a time, they walked to meet their man.

Kat watched Badger's face, noting the shock, almost the terror, as he glanced at the other men, wondering what was going on. She watched as all the men looked at each other and then locked gazes with the special woman coming toward each of them.

As she got close, she said, "Badger?"

"Yes?" he asked, his voice cautious.

"Do you love me?"

He nodded. "You know I do."

She smiled. "You know I love you, right?"

He nodded his head slowly. "Yes, I do."

She smiled, reached out a hand and asked, "Will you marry me?"

His jaw dropped, and he glanced at the other men. She stole a glance to see how the others were doing. She wanted to laugh at the shock on this row of men's faces, but it was no longer a laughing matter.

This meant everything to her.

Kat studied Badger's gaze, seeing the puzzle pieces fall into place, the women in their dresses, the matching colors on their men, the women all lined up, reaching out hands to their partners. Badger glanced around as she stepped up to his side and gently turned him to face the minister.

She reached a finger to his lips. "The only thing you need to know is if you love me. And the only thing I need to tell you is how much I love you."

He couldn't speak.

She watched his Adam's apple slide up and down his throat as he tried to clear it.

She said, "You don't have to say a word. Well, you will in a minute, but right now you just have to nod your head."

He smiled, picked up her fingers, kissed the top of them and whispered, "Yes."

And just like every other pair in the row, they faced the minister as he intoned, "Dear friends and family, we are gathered here today ..."

Kat's heart was overwhelmed with joy and peace, knowing she had done the right thing. She went through the ceremony in a daze. Her heart opened as each couple's names were called out and as each made their vows.

As the justice of the peace asked for the rings, Levi

stepped up and, one by one, handed out the rings each had chosen.

When Badger took one look at the plain titanium ring, he smiled, and when he saw the ivory piece braided through it and her matching ivory ring with the titanium inlay, he sighed happily. "How did you know?" he asked in a daze.

She held out her hand as he put the ring on her left ring finger, and she smiled. "You know? The one thing I can tell you for sure right now is that I do know who you are, Badger, on the inside and on the outside."

Just then the justice of the peace said, "And now you may kiss the bride."

Badger drew her gently toward him and whispered, "Thank God," and he kissed her, and it wasn't a gentle sealing-his-vows kiss, and it definitely wasn't a kiss for public display. It was a heated and possessive *you're mine now* kiss.

And she couldn't be happier.

The crowd broke out in cheers.

BADGER WAS STILL in a daze. He didn't quite understand how any of this had come to pass. When he'd turned to see Kat walking toward him in that absolutely beautiful dress, her floral bouquet matching the color of his tie, he'd finally understood why Levi had asked them to all wear these colors. And Badger realized just how much effort had gone into making this happen. He looked around at all his buddies, every one of them looking just as dazed, and yet just as happy as he was.

Erick caught his gaze, lifted his shoulders as if to say, *How did they pull this off?*

Badger knew the bewilderment in his own gaze was just as evident. But not one of them was willing to take their arm off the woman they held close. He glanced down at Kat, his arms still wrapped around her shoulders and said, "I don't know how you did this, but thank you."

She brushed a finger gently across his lips and whispered, "Thank you."

He kissed her yet again. "And I thought it all had to do with Levi."

Just then Alfred and Jim grabbed several men in the crowd, and, within minutes, the tables were set up and heavily ladened with fancy wedding ceremony food. The crowd was still cheering and clapping, Dotty was barking, and the music was still playing, but Badger was numb to it all. He couldn't believe his luck that he had found somebody who would love him as he was and would want to spend her life with him.

She wrapped her arms around him and seemed so content to be here with him.

Kat smiled and said, "Levi and Ice were a huge help."

Badger turned to look for Ice, who was wearing this minuscule gold dress that made her legs look like stilts. She stood beside Levi, a smile on her face, almost a tear in her eyes, and she looked young and absolutely ravishing.

"She looks stunning, doesn't she?" Badger asked.

"They both do," Kat admitted. "If there was ever a couple who needed to be together ..."

And, as they watched their friends, Levi turned, dropped to one knee, and the crowd fell completely silent. He held out his hand and lifted a ring box. Ice stared at him as everyone gasped. But the gasps of joy were muted because nobody wanted to miss hearing her answer. She looked at

Levi with such shock on her face that Badger wondered if maybe Levi had overestimated this moment. Badger's heart constricted in pain for the man who'd always been there for them.

Kat leaned forward and whispered, "Looks like Levi had his own agenda."

Badger shook his head, not daring to speak and miss the moment.

Ice unfroze just then and shouted, "Yes," and she threw her arms around Levi, and the guests erupted in more cheers. Levi stood, captured Ice in his arms and swung her around before lowering her to her feet and kissing her passionately.

Shocked and delighted, Badger hugged Kat close and whispered, "Did you see that coming?"

Kat stared at her husband in a daze. "No," she said. "I had no clue."

Badger chuckled. "Looks like Levi had the last surprise after all."

And Badger tugged Kat to him and kissed her yet again.

This concludes Book 8 of SEALs of Steel: The Final Reveal.

Read about Ethan: The K9 Files, Book 1

THE K9 FILES: ETHAN BOOK 1

When one door closes ... second chances open another ...

Ethan was lost after a major accident abruptly shifted him from a military life to a civilian one, from working with dogs to odd jobs ... In that time, he'd spent months healing from his physical injuries. When he connects with Badger and the rest of his Titanium Corp. group of former SEALs, Badger offers Ethan an opportunity he can't refuse. A chance to do the work he used to do ... with a twist.

Cinnamon works from home as a project manager plus is heavily involved in global dog rescues—dogs of all kinds. When Ethan walks into the next door's vet's office with an injured shepherd in his arms, she sees another lost soul—just like the canine ones she helps.

Ethan knows he's about to take a dangerous step, but he's on the job, and no one—on the job or not—hurts animals while he's around. This poor shepherd has taken enough abuse, and Ethan fears she is only the tip of a nightmare he's determined to uncover. But he knows she's going to lead him in the right direction.

He has his sights set on saving one dog in particular, Sentry: K9 File 01.

Book 1 is available now!

To find out more visit Dale Mayer's website.

http://smarturl.it/EthanDMUniversal

Author's Note

Thank you for reading The Final Reveal: SEALs of Steel, Book 8! If you enjoyed the book, please take a moment and leave a short review.

Dear reader,

I love to hear from readers, and you can contact me at my website: www.dalemayer.com or at my Facebook author page. To be informed of new releases and special offers, sign up for my newsletter or follow me on BookBub. And if you are interested in joining Dale Mayer's Reader Group, here is the Facebook sign up page.
facebook.com/groups/402384989872660

Cheers,
Dale Mayer

Your THREE Free Books Are Waiting!

Grab your copy of SEALs of Honor Books 1 – 3 for free!

Meet Mason, Hawk and Dane. *Brave, badass warriors who serve their country with honor and love their women to the limits of life and death.*

DOWNLOAD your copy right now! Just tell me where to send it.

www.smarturl.it/DaleHonorFreeBundle

About the Author

Dale Mayer is a USA Today bestselling author best known for her Psychic Visions and Family Blood Ties series. Her contemporary romances are raw and full of passion and emotion (Second Chances, SKIN), her thrillers will keep you guessing (By Death series), and her romantic comedies will keep you giggling (It's a Dog's Life and Charmin Marvin Romantic Comedy series).

She honors the stories that come to her – and some of them are crazy and break all the rules and cross multiple genres!

To go with her fiction, she also writes nonfiction in many different fields with books available on resume writing, companion gardening and the US mortgage system. She has recently published her Career Essentials Series. All her books are available in print and ebook format.

Connect with Dale Mayer Online

Dale's Website – www.dalemayer.com
Twitter – @DaleMayer
Facebook – dalemayer.com/fb
BookBub – bookbub.com/authors/dale-mayer

Also by Dale Mayer

Published Adult Books:

The K9 Files
Ethan, Book 1
Pierce, Book 2

Lovely Lethal Gardens
Arsenic in the Azaleas, Book 1
Bones in the Begonias, Book 2
Corpse in the Carnations, Book 3
Daggers in the Dahlias, Book 4
Evidence in the Echinacea, Book 5
Footprints in the Ferns, Book 6

Psychic Vision Series
Tuesday's Child
Hide 'n Go Seek
Maddy's Floor
Garden of Sorrow
Knock Knock...
Rare Find
Eyes to the Soul
Now You See Her
Shattered
Into the Abyss
Seeds of Malice

Eye of the Falcon
Itsy-Bitsy Spider
Unmasked
Deep Beneath
Psychic Visions Books 1–3
Psychic Visions Books 4–6
Psychic Visions Books 7–9

By Death Series
Touched by Death
Haunted by Death
Chilled by Death
By Death Books 1–3

Broken Protocols – Romantic Comedy Series
Cat's Meow
Cat's Pajamas
Cat's Cradle
Cat's Claus
Broken Protocols 1-4

Broken and... Mending
Skin
Scars
Scales (of Justice)
Broken but... Mending 1-3

Glory
Genesis
Tori
Celeste
Glory Trilogy

Biker Blues

Morgan: Biker Blues, Volume 1
Cash: Biker Blues, Volume 2

SEALs of Honor

Mason: SEALs of Honor, Book 1
Hawk: SEALs of Honor, Book 2
Dane: SEALs of Honor, Book 3
Swede: SEALs of Honor, Book 4
Shadow: SEALs of Honor, Book 5
Cooper: SEALs of Honor, Book 6
Markus: SEALs of Honor, Book 7
Evan: SEALs of Honor, Book 8
Mason's Wish: SEALs of Honor, Book 9
Chase: SEALs of Honor, Book 10
Brett: SEALs of Honor, Book 11
Devlin: SEALs of Honor, Book 12
Easton: SEALs of Honor, Book 13
Ryder: SEALs of Honor, Book 14
Macklin: SEALs of Honor, Book 15
Corey: SEALs of Honor, Book 16
Warrick: SEALs of Honor, Book 17
Tanner: SEALs of Honor, Book 18
Jackson: SEALs of Honor, Book 19
Kanen: SEALs of Honor, Book 20
Nelson: SEALs of Honor, Book 21
SEALs of Honor, Books 1–3
SEALs of Honor, Books 4–6
SEALs of Honor, Books 7–10
SEALs of Honor, Books 11–13
SEALs of Honor, Books 14–16
SEALs of Honor, Books 17–19

Heroes for Hire

Levi's Legend: Heroes for Hire, Book 1

Stone's Surrender: Heroes for Hire, Book 2

Merk's Mistake: Heroes for Hire, Book 3

Rhodes's Reward: Heroes for Hire, Book 4

Flynn's Firecracker: Heroes for Hire, Book 5

Logan's Light: Heroes for Hire, Book 6

Harrison's Heart: Heroes for Hire, Book 7

Saul's Sweetheart: Heroes for Hire, Book 8

Dakota's Delight: Heroes for Hire, Book 9

Michael's Mercy (Part of Sleeper SEAL Series)

Tyson's Treasure: Heroes for Hire, Book 10

Jace's Jewel: Heroes for Hire, Book 11

Rory's Rose: Heroes for Hire, Book 12

Brandon's Bliss: Heroes for Hire, Book 13

Liam's Lily: Heroes for Hire, Book 14

North's Nikki: Heroes for Hire, Book 15

Anders's Angel: Heroes for Hire, Book 16

Reyes's Raina: Heroes for Hire, Book 17

Dezi's Diamond: Heroes for Hire, Book 18

Vince's Vixen: Heroes for Hire, Book 19

Heroes for Hire, Books 1–3

Heroes for Hire, Books 4–6

Heroes for Hire, Books 7–9

SEALs of Steel

Badger: SEALs of Steel, Book 1

Erick: SEALs of Steel, Book 2

Cade: SEALs of Steel, Book 3

Talon: SEALs of Steel, Book 4

Laszlo: SEALs of Steel, Book 5

Geir: SEALs of Steel, Book 6

Jager: SEALs of Steel, Book 7
The Final Reveal: SEALs of Steel, Book 8

Collections
Dare to Be You…
Dare to Love…
Dare to be Strong…
RomanceX3

Standalone Novellas
It's a Dog's Life
Riana's Revenge
Second Chances

Published Young Adult Books:

Family Blood Ties Series
Vampire in Denial
Vampire in Distress
Vampire in Design
Vampire in Deceit
Vampire in Defiance
Vampire in Conflict
Vampire in Chaos
Vampire in Crisis
Vampire in Control
Vampire in Charge
Family Blood Ties Set 1–3
Family Blood Ties Set 1–5
Family Blood Ties Set 4–6
Family Blood Ties Set 7–9
Sian's Solution, A Family Blood Ties Series Prequel

Novelette

Design series
Dangerous Designs
Deadly Designs
Darkest Designs
Design Series Trilogy

Standalone
In Cassie's Corner
Gem Stone (a Gemma Stone Mystery)
Time Thieves

Published Non-Fiction Books:

Career Essentials
Career Essentials: The Résumé
Career Essentials: The Cover Letter
Career Essentials: The Interview
Career Essentials: 3 in 1

Printed in Great Britain
by Amazon